The
Case Against
My Brother

Libby Sternberg

bancroft press Baltimore, Maryland

Published by Bancroft Press ("Books that enlighten")
P.O. Box 65360, Baltimore, MD 21209
800-637-7377
410-764-1967 (fax)
www.bancroftpress.com

Cover and interior design: Tammy Sneath Grimes, Crescent Communications
www.tsgcrescent.com • 814.941.7447

Author photo: Beltrami Studio, Rutland, VT

ISBN 1-890862-51-7(cloth)
EAN 978-1-890862-51-0 (cloth)
LCCN 2007936856 (cloth)

ISBN 1-890862-54-1 (paper)
EAN 978-1-890862-54-1 (paper)

Printed in the United States of America

First Edition

1 3 5 7 9 10 8 6 4 2

In memory of my father, born Casimir Malinowski, who changed his last name (and mine) to Malin when I was young

Chapter One

FALL 1922

"Matuski!"

Officer Miller's voice sounded like a bark in the warm night.

My heart racing, I pretended he had the wrong fellow and kept walking down Portland's Burnside Avenue, one foot in front of the other. *Don't look, don't look, don't look . . . Steady, steady . . .*

"Turn around, you dumb Polack!"

My fists clenched at that, but still I wouldn't turn. I wouldn't give him the satisfaction.

An arched alley entry—a shadowy hole—loomed on my right. My breath came fast but his footfalls were faster. I had to lose him, had to keep him off my trail. I couldn't lead him to Adam. Just a few more steps . . .

"Hold it there, or I'll—"

His words died as I ducked into the dark entrance. It smelled of moss and damp walls, of something foul and slimy. A sharp vine tugged at my sleeve, but I pulled away. I held my breath and sped to a backyard garden. Beyond that, I'd find an alley, and then I could race off.

No! He saw me, and he was still following me. Just as I made my way into the yard, I heard him cursing and muttering. I imagined him bumping his head on the arched wall, his pace slowed by the thorny vine grabbing his coat. It made me smile.

I looked left and right—nothing but yards and alley—and all more open than the street itself. *Crap!* I'd mucked up. I no longer had time to scamper away. He'd be in the yard soon, and I'd be an easy catch.

My throat dried up and I couldn't swallow. My fists clenched and unclenched as I kept looking this way and that, hoping I'd spot a safe haven. What would I say when he asked why I was out and about so late? I had to have an excuse—why hadn't I thought of that? What was the matter with me? Panic crawled up my chest and knotted my thoughts. If Adam were here, he'd know what to say.

A cat screeched out a meow of surprise and Officer Miller cursed again. The feline skittered into the open and then up onto and above an old rickety porch. There! That was a safe place! I grabbed hold of the splintery wood and followed, speedily hoisting myself up. My hand scraped along the planking's jagged edge and I felt moist blood bead under my coat. It didn't matter. I lay flat and still, looking through the porch boards' thin slits at Officer Miller's hat below.

I held my breath.

He scratched his head, pushing up the bill of his hat. "Matuski?" he called out, but his voice wasn't so strong anymore. A light went on in a house across the alley. Officer Miller's head turned in that direction, but he stayed put. He sighed and stomped a foot. He took off his hat and smoothed back his hair.

And then, at long last, he left, heading out the way he came, though more slowly and carefully this time. I counted each step until I couldn't hear another one. And then I forced myself to wait a good minute or two to be sure the coast was clear.

I stretched, climbed over the porch railing, and crouched before jumping. *Ouch!* My ankle throbbed from the fall. I brushed off the pain and went into the alley, looking up and down, staring into the darkness. Nothing.

At last, I ran.

It felt good to run, each step leaving something behind—worry, pain, sadness. My breath came fast, and the soft *clump-clomp* of my feet masked all other sounds. Feeling like the only man alive, I barreled through the city's dark byways as if a fire-breathing monster were on my tail. My lungs burned for air. My legs throbbed for rest. But I ran on and on and it still felt good.

I ran toward the East, where pink shreds of clouds shyly lit Portland's sky, signaling dawn's arrival. I thundered forward—East toward what used to be home.

Glancing behind me again, I ran on into the cool shadows, down Burnside, south on Fifth, left on Yamhill. I ran past parked Tin Lizzies, Buicks, and Studebakers crammed up against the curb near what my Uncle Pete called a "house of ill repute." There, music and noise floated into the silent city. Someone was playing a popular new tune on a tinny piano—"Carolina in the Morning"—while boozy voices crooned the words:

Nothing could be finer than to be in Carolina in the morning
Nothing could be sweeter than my sweetie when I meet her in
the morning . . .

Carolina wasn't home, but it *was* back East. Homesickness choked me.

My steps echoed on empty streets that smelled of wet pine and fuel oil from ships anchored in Portland's harbor. East, East, East—how I wished I could keep running all the way across the country, over mountains, flat prairies, gentle hills, all the way to the city of my birth, to another harbor that smelled of humid life, to a place, unlike Portland, where at least I had a few friends and a pocketful of fond memories, and where I blended in, like everyone else in a crowd.

I didn't want to be here in Portland. Whenever I found myself walking or running East, my pace quickened and my energy soared. It was as if home were just over the horizon.

Though the air was cooler now, the sweat on my brow kept my hair slicked down under my cap. As I neared the house I was looking for, I slowed my pace. I looked right and left. No sign of a policeman on the beat. No police cars, either.

Nobody, in fact, to see me walking toward the corner house, where one yellow rectangle of light lit up an upper floor.

He was up and waiting.

After looking up and down the street again, I made three quick raps on the front door, followed by two slow raps—that was the signal. I saw the light upstairs flick off, and a shade move ever so slightly in the ashy dark. Then, a few seconds later, I heard the slow creak of the door as he pulled it open.

"You've got to get out of here," I whispered before I even saw his face. "Miller knows you're here."

Adam didn't say a word. As he ran back upstairs, I listened to his ascending footsteps. A few moments later, he returned, this time opening the door fully. Stepping out into the early morning with me, my brother shrugged into an old tweed jacket and placed on his head a flat tan cap that looked a lot like mine. Our mother had bought them through the Montgomery Ward catalog the year before she'd died.

As we walked down the street together, he shifted his small bundle of clothes to his left hand so he could tousle my head with his right. I pulled away. Adam was two years older than me, but I was fifteen, not some pup.

"You shouldn't be out so late," he said, and I could hear the smile in his voice even through the shadows. "Does Pete know?"

"He thinks I'm sleeping," I said.

"Until he checks on you."

"He won't check." Our Uncle Pete was a sound sleeper, and never one to worry about us when we were out of sight. But he'd be rising soon to start delivering milk. I had to time my return so as not to run into him as he left for the day.

I looked behind me. Though the street was still clear, I picked up my pace. I thought I heard a car engine rumble to life in the distance. The neighborhood was quiet, but lights were flickering on in a few houses. We passed a big brown house, where I heard women's laughter tinkling into the night. If this was a bad area, police might not be far behind. We had to hurry. Adam, seemingly unconcerned about getting caught, looked at my pockets, even reaching out to pat one.

"I thought you were bringing . . ."

"Oh, yeah, I forgot." I pulled a cloth-wrapped roll from my right pocket, and Adam grabbed it, unwrapping it and greedily tearing off a portion with his teeth.

"This all?"

"There's more at Pete's." We turned a corner and I touched him lightly on the shoulder. "C'mon, we gotta hurry. He'll be up soon." I started running again, but Adam lagged behind as he focused on eating his "breakfast." At a corner a half block away, I turned back and stage-whispered "C'mon!" as I waited for him to catch up.

"All right, all right," he said in a low voice. Finishing the roll, he wiped away stray crumbs from his mouth, then hefted his bundle over one shoulder. Joining me at the corner of Ash, he pointed toward the river and the shipping yards. "There's an empty office at Beely's Sawmill," he said. "They're closed now. I could hide out there."

"I was thinking you could come home tonight—I get my newspaper money after today's route," I said, already starting to feel disappointed and afraid. It was as if Adam thought this was all a big joke, as if he didn't fully realize the trouble he was in.

Reinforcing my view, he laughed. "Home? That's the first place Miller'll look for me, kid!"

I shook my head. "Don't call me 'kid.'"

He looked at me through narrowed eyes, his mouth tugging into a smile. "Sure thing," he said. "Scrawny."

I would have punched him, but it would just waste time. He knew calling me that was a sore point with me. Yeah, I was skinny and tall, shooting up so fast Pete complained about having to buy me new clothes "every week," but I could take care of myself most of the time. At least I hoped I could. Adam was forcing me to.

I let my hands unclench. "Miller won't look for you at home. He follows me. That's how he figured out you were at the Third Street house. But home? He'd never guess I brought you there. He's not following us now." I shoved my hands into my pockets and shivered. Now that we'd stopped, my sweat clamped on my face and body like ice. The weather wasn't yet cold, but the early morning run had left me damp as a dish rag.

I looked at Adam, waiting for him to see the wisdom of my plan. Staying out in the open was an invitation to trouble. If I could get him home, he'd be safe—at least for a few hours. I'd do my afternoon paper route, get my monthly pay from my boss, then hand it over to Adam so he could hop a train and get out of town. Sure, I might take a whipping from Pete for "losing" the money, but Adam would get safely away.

Adam smiled, his wide mouth lifting his face into that happy-go-lucky grin, which usually made me feel like neither of us had a trouble in the world. But today, it annoyed me. In fact, I again felt like punching him—this time to wake him up to the trouble he was in.

"Smart thinking, Carl. But Miller's no dope. He might come

over again."

"You can hide in the cellar, near the furnace—in the coal bin if you have to."

He laughed. "And be black as old Thomas?" Thomas was the Negro Street Araber who sold fruits and vegetables from the back of his horse-drawn cart. "That would be a good disguise."

Before I had a chance to argue, Adam gave in. "All right," he said. "I'm too tired to fight. At least I can get more food at home." He reached out to rub my head again, but I pulled away, walking ahead of him.

The pink and orange strips grew in the Eastern sky, bathing the area in an eerie gray light. Dawn was drifting in with the tide, and soon the city would be bustling with traffic, noise, and work. Pete would be up and on his route by now, so it would be safe to sneak home, as long as Officer Miller didn't catch us.

"Come on!" I shouted to Adam, sounding as angry as I felt. Without looking back, I took off running. In a second, I heard him following me, and then, as he passed, he showed me a toothy smile. A race!

No longer angry, I laughed and began sprinting, struggling to catch up.

Chapter Two

Adam and I were orphaned last year. Our dad died before I knew him, and our mother passed away from a bad lung fourteen months ago—fourteen months and five days ago, to be exact.

That's when Adam took charge of things, deciding where we should go and how we should get there. He's the one who decided we should head West from Baltimore—out to our uncle's house in Oregon. If it had been left to me, we'd have been starving on Baltimore streets to this day. Adam told me the house wasn't ours—Ma didn't own it, he said—and we had to move on.

It was a lot of change to go through all at once, and sometimes I'm not sure I remember everything in the right order or what was real and what was a dream.

During those first few months after Ma died, I was half-expecting somebody to tell me *that* was a mistake. I even dreamt it that way the night before her funeral. I dreamt I went downstairs in our Baltimore rowhouse and heard someone in the kitchen. Grabbing my baseball bat to ward off an intruder, I'd crept down to the basement kitchen, only to see my mother smiling at me as she stirred a pot on the stove. She looked happy and lively, her brown hair pulled into a bun at her neck, her big white apron covering a dark dress. She looked healthy, the way she'd been before getting sick.

"What you carry that bat for, *syneczku?*" she asked me, using the Polish for "little son" as if I were still a baby.

"I'm not a kid anymore, Ma," I said, irritated, but irritation warmed to anger, anger to regret, and I awakened to the sound of rain on the window, feeling as if my bad temper had chased Ma away forever.

Shortly before my mother passed on, she looked at both Adam and me across the kitchen table and said, "You look after your brother." I figured she was talking to Adam, because he was the older one. But lately I couldn't shake the feeling that maybe she'd been talking to me, too, telling me to help Adam when his easygoing ways got him into trouble.

Adam helped me the day of the funeral, telling me what to wear and how to act, handing me a big white handkerchief before we went into St. Stanislaus's—just in case I got the sniffles or something, he said. He even poked fun at me, telling me my pants were too short and I looked like I'd grabbed somebody else's clothes to wear.

He didn't get the sniffles and neither did I—even when the priest handed Adam Ma's rosary, which he then gave to me. I kept thinking how my ankles poked out of my pants legs, and I wondered if we would have enough money to buy a new pair.

There wasn't enough money for anything.

After the funeral Mass and burial, Adam sat in our basement kitchen and told me we'd have to move.

"We have an uncle in Portland, you know," he said quietly. "Pete Cyzska is Ma's brother—our uncle. I've written to him."

I couldn't believe it at first. I asked him a lot of questions, but I was only fourteen back then and didn't know anything. He told me that everything in the house was already sold—he'd seen to it right before Ma died. He told me we needed the money to pay off her debts, but there wasn't enough to cover all of them. If we didn't want to go to jail, we had to get out of town.

Jail? I was unhappy enough in school. But I had friends in Baltimore. There was Billy Petrovnov, my best friend, who played ball with me every summer in Patterson Park. There was Julian Grekowski, who was always bragging about how he was going to be president one day. We called him "President Julie," which made his ears turn red. And there was even Esther Krawiec, who wore the prettiest, cleanest dresses to Mass, and whose mother baked cookies and cakes that Esther shared with me but not the other boys.

Friends and the familiar were hard to give up, but the threat of jail made me break out into a sweat. I wanted to leave that instant. We didn't leave until a few days later, though, and each day in the house after that talk, I felt like a fugitive, afraid of the meekest knock on the door.

Just before we left, Adam bought me a pair of new pants that fit right.

Then he bought our train tickets and we headed West. Once clear of Maryland, I could breathe again. They'd never find us now, I thought. By the time we reached Chicago, though, I began to think that leaving Baltimore and heading west wasn't such a great adventure, and homesickness tightly gripped my heart.

The west was supposed to be a place full of cowboys and excitement. But it's not—at least as far as I could tell from the train. It's just empty and hot and a kind of lonely that makes you feel scooped out inside, like you're always hungry and nothing satisfies.

We had to switch trains several times, in big, echoing stations bustling with people who looked like they knew where they were going. Adam seemed to be one of them.

I stayed close to Adam the whole way. He made sure we had food—not much, but enough to keep hunger pangs at bay. He cheered me by poking fun at some of the passengers. He led with confidence even when he wasn't sure which train we needed to be on, and I kept thinking if I could be half the man he was, I'd be sure of my place in the world. And as long as Adam was around, I'd felt safe. He had taken Ma's words to heart, looking after me in ways big and small.

He was always there, nudging me forward with a "here you go, Carl."

Here you go, Carl, this is our train.

Here you go, Carl, a fresh apple and some coffee.

Here you go, Carl, Uncle Pete's house is up this street.

Adam, Pete, and I all lived together now in a rickety bungalow near the river. Portland's nearly a hundred miles inland from the sea, so it hardly seems like a real seaport to me. But it's supposed to be a busy one. I don't know. Nothing seems as busy or as big as what we left back East.

Once we'd arrived at Pete's last year, I was happy to be done with traveling. But now not a day goes by that I don't think of traveling home.

It became a dream of mine to save up enough money to go back East, where things happen, where the air smells like people do things—not as empty as it did here—and maybe even to pay off the last of the family debts and buy back our little home near the harbor. Working together, Adam and I could do it, and he agreed. Without Adam knowing it, I even wrote a letter to Esther a couple months ago, telling her we were going to come back. That was before Adam got into trouble.

Adam had been working odd jobs since we came to Oregon, but Pete wanted me to go to school. I did a year at St. Clare's but could hardly wait to get out. First off, Pete had to work a double shift, and still had to scrimp to pay the tuition. And I was the oldest kid in my class, which made me feel even more like the odd fellow out. I talked Pete into letting me drop it this year. I was eager to get to work.

I had two jobs: I delivered newspapers, and I worked a few hours each day at St. Mary's Academy. The handyman there, Lester, was teaching me how to repair things. Pete knew Lester from church and got me the job. I wished Adam had found a regular job like that. It might have saved us from the trouble we were in.

You see, a month or so ago, Adam hooked up with a plumbing outfit on Yamhill Road. They sent him out to a house in the hills on the west side of town to fix some leaky kitchen pipes for the Peterson family.

Adam had always been a good-looking kid—not like me. I was thin and pale, and nothing to boast about. Adam was tall and dark-haired with a great smile that melted the hearts of everyone who met him, like Rose, the daughter in that swanky Peterson household. Adam talked her into sneaking away and meeting him for a night on the town at least twice, until her parents caught on and forbade her to ever see him again.

Adam wasn't too upset, though. He just said he had to be more careful. "Her parents'll come around," he told me when he arrived home late one night, smelling like fancy perfume. "She's going to talk them into it. And just you wait, then, Carl. We'll be on Easy Street."

Easy Street? Hah! Adam had this crazy idea he could actually marry this girl, after which her parents would set him up for life. That dream came to a crashing end, however, when the Peterson family was reported burglarized, and some jewelry stolen by the burglar—a diamond bracelet, a pearl pin, and a couple pairs of ruby earrings. The stuff was worth a pretty penny, and whoever took it had to know the house and where the jewelry had been hidden—had to know the family even had the stuff.

That's why Adam was in trouble. The girl's father told the

police "some Polish papist" stole the jewelry. That was three days ago, and Adam had been on the run ever since.

"Papist" is a word I'd never heard before coming to Portland. Back in Baltimore, it seemed like everybody was a Catholic. But here, I'd heard some folks at St. Mary's complaining about a "campaign against Catholics."

Pete was upset about all this "papist" talk. He sometimes went to meetings about it, and when he came home, he never looked happy. I wanted to find out more so I could help him—but first, I had to dig Adam out of his hole.

———

Adam sat calmly at Pete's kitchen table. He looked serene, as if he were thinking about what pleasurable thing he wanted to do that day—go fishing, meet up with some friends, or just sit in a chair reading a book. He didn't look like a fellow who was on the run. I was more worried than he was.

"Not going to work today?" Adam asked me. He held a knife in one hand and a round of cheese in the other.

"They can get on without me," I said, staring out the window, onto a backyard and dirt alley between Pete's house and the next house in the neighborhood. Most of all, though, I was looking out for Miller.

"Watch it, or they *will* get on without you."

Quickly, I turned toward him and said, "If the Academy doesn't want me anymore, I'll do odd jobs, just like you."

He snorted a laugh. "Regular work is better than what I do, kid."

"Don't call me 'kid,'" I said. "I can make my way on my own." But as soon as I said it, the untruth in it seemed to light up the room. I'd needed Adam's help when we traveled west, and I didn't think I could face the return trip without him. He probably knew it, too. My face warmed as I waited for a retort. But none came. Instead, he cut off a large chunk of cheese and ate in silence for awhile.

And then, as if he'd read my mind, he started talking about going home. Pointing the knife at me, he said, "In Baltimore, you should look into going back to school. You always were a good student."

"I didn't do so well last year," I said. It had been a tough year in a tough school—mostly Italian kids, and I was the only newcomer.

"That was different," Adam said, waving the knife. "Before that, you were always bringing home the good grades. Not like me."

He was right. While Adam had barely made it through school each year, I easily passed my classes, hardly needing to study in order to score high grades. It was like our faults and assets had been precisely divided between us, with no overlap. He was good-looking and charming, while I was plain and shy. I was a good student and obedient, while he struggled at learning and behaving.

But I envied even his faults because they seemed so much better than my strengths. He might have seemed tactless and shallow to some, always poking fun at people and events he had nothing to do with, but that was part of his charm—he could take something heavy and sad and make it seem light as air and more than bearable. I didn't have that gift. If not for his charm, I would have spent the past year a hopeless mope.

As for his other big fault, he'd gotten into a few scrapes before the Peterson problem, but nothing serious. He'd broken a window with a baseball once in Baltimore, but it had been an honest mistake. And he'd soaped up Mr. Warton's store windows one

Halloween, but only because old Warton had been mean to us kids who stopped by after school. At his core, Adam was a good boy with a good heart. It bothered me when others didn't see him that way.

As I studied my brother now, I wondered why he couldn't turn all his good points into something better, why he couldn't take the good advice he gave me and use it for himself. He thought having a "regular" job was a good thing, yet he didn't go after one. He picked up work here and there. Even Pete had told him more than once that he should find something permanent. Yet Adam was the one who'd gotten me the newspaper delivery job with cranky Gus Winston. Adam had told me I'd like it, that it would make me feel like a man to be earning regular money. If that worked for me, why didn't it also work for him?

Gus Winston hadn't wanted to hire me at first. He'd made some comment about my last name, saying "Matuski" sounded "Bolshevik" to him and he didn't want "none of those radical foreigners" handling a route in a proper neighborhood. But Adam, who could be pretty menacing when he wanted to be, stared down at squat Gus, saying, "You don't hire this kid and nobody in this neighborhood buys the paper. You can count on it." Gus said I'd do until he found someone better. I don't think he ever tried.

Adam looked out for me without me asking him to. Maybe that was the problem. He used up all his best parts helping me and didn't have much left for himself. All the more reason for me to pitch in for him now.

"If we find the real thief, this will all go away," I said to him, still keeping a lookout for Miller. What I didn't add was that we could then go back to planning our trip back home.

Adam shook his head. "They want me, kid. They've already decided whose name is on this crime."

"Come on, Adam, we can figure this out together. And then

you're home free." What I meant was we would both be home free, really home—away from Portland.

After eating some more cheese and bread, he stood and got himself a glass of water. Wiping his mouth on his sleeve, he leaned against the porcelain sink. "You're a smart one," he said, "but this is beyond you."

I let the insult slide by. "We can do it together. You just have to tell me things about the Petersons and then I'll follow up with—"

"Tell you *what*? What do I know?"

"Like who knew about the jewelry," I said, irritation raising my voice.

Crossing his arms over his chest, he shook his head, didn't look at me, and said nothing.

"Damn it, Adam, who knew about the jewelry?" I repeated.

Grimacing, he shot me a look. "Pete'll wash your mouth out if you keep up that kind of talk."

"You talk that way. So does Lester at the Academy. So does Pete."

Adam laughed. "Yeah, and look how far we've gotten."

I brushed past his concern for my language and returned to the question. "C'mon, Adam. Think. Who knew about the jewels? That's the first step."

"Everybody knew about them!" His good humor left him and he strode to the back door and stared out. "Everybody in the world—at least everybody in the house. Rose's parents, her brothers," he mumbled. "Stupid jewelry. They probably have a cartload left, and they're crying like it was a favorite son they lost."

I ignored his bitterness and pressed on with my questions. "Who exactly owned it? Was it Rose's?"

"Nope. Her mother's. Something she inherited." He ran his fingers through his hair. "Rose showed it to me one day."

"How many brothers does she have?"

"Two. One's married and lives in Irvington," he said. Irvington was a posh area of town. It fit. "The other's just ten."

"The married one visit a lot?"

"I don't know."

"They visit any time before the stuff went missing?" I asked.

"I don't know, Carl. I was never really invited into the family circle, you know." He shifted his weight from one foot to the other and turned to me. "Look, this is useless. You won't figure this out. The best thing is for me to just get away, at least 'til things cool down. How long before you get that cash from Gus?"

"Not 'til this afternoon." Adam knew the Academy wouldn't pay me for another week, so he didn't bother to ask about that check. Besides, I could cheat Pete out of my newspaper money, but I knew he counted on using some of my Academy pay for rent and food. I didn't think Adam would want me denying our uncle his due.

"When?"

"Well, I usually pick up my papers after school, at the Jasluzek store. Gus'll be there with my pay."

Adam, apparently relieved, walked toward the stairs. "I'm going to catch some sleep. Wake me up before you go, kid."

Chapter Three

While Adam slept, I felt on edge, waiting for the cops to come around or Pete to come home early.

I should have been at the Academy working. Despite my bravado around Adam, I felt guilty letting Lester down. I knew he was repainting an office today, and I would have made the task go twice as fast for him. Not being there meant I'd be docked for a day's pay, too.

Oh, heck, I'd get over to the Academy, help out Lester, and be back before anyone stumbled onto Adam. With Officer Miller sure he was still on the lam, Adam was safe sleeping off his troubles at Pete's for the day. We'd plot out his next move after he was rested. So I struck out into the morning, heading on Fifth Avenue toward the school.

It was a bright day with just a hint of autumn in the air. I didn't need my jacket, so I took it off and held it with one finger over my shoulder. My cap I kept on because it cut down the glare of the sun.

The walk gave me time to think. If Adam was too beat up inside to help figure out who the real thief was, I'd have to do it as best I could on my own. Maybe he was just tired—tired of always being the one in charge.

Even before Ma passed away, Adam had helped out. He

helped her in the corner store where she worked, filling in for her when she was sick. He delivered newspapers after school. He fixed meals for us when she was bedridden, and paid the bills, sweet-talking more than one creditor into accepting payments late. He made sure I did my schoolwork and got me a new pair of shoes when my old ones cramped my toes. Sometimes, it seemed like he could do anything. If I needed something, Adam got it for me. Now it was my turn to return the favor.

Rose told Adam she had two brothers. The young one might be ten, but he still might have done it. I'd known kids who played craps before school for pennies. If he lost a lot, the brother would have run up big debts and might have needed the jewelry to pawn for some easy cash. If he'd been home at the time of the robbery, he was a possibility. I wouldn't rule him out just because he was a kid.

And then there was the older, married brother living in Irving-ton. He could need cash for any number of things. If he was des-perate, nabbing some of his mother's jewelry could solve a lot of problems pretty easily.

There had to be others as well—tradesmen and repairmen, maybe even a maid or butler. Or maybe it had just been a lucky burglar, breaking into the house to steal it clean, hearing some-thing that made him hurry, grabbing the first shiny things that caught his eyes.

As I put together my list of possibilities, my muscles relaxed and some of my worry lifted. It felt good to be walking on this beautiful day. When the sun was shining and the air was a warm touch on my brow, it was easy to think that all problems could be solved by reasonable people getting together and talking. I started building a dream—one where I figured out who the real thief was, after which the Petersons were so mortified at accusing Adam that they paid him a generous reward. We'd take the extra cash and head eastward before the weather turned cool. The sky, a washed-out blue decorated with wisps of clouds, made it easy to nourish dreams like that, and by the time I got to the Academy, I was actually whistling an upbeat tune.

But then something caught my eye: a broadside tacked to a telephone pole, sending a hot rush of indignation from my head to my feet.

"SISTER LUCRETIA, AN ESCAPED NUN, TO TALK OF HER FEARFUL EXPERIENCES!" it read in big block letters. It advertised an event at the public school auditorium downtown. "Sister Lucretia" was going to inform the good citizens of Portland, as she'd done in other great cities in the land, of the "frightful rituals" and "perversions of flesh and spirit" that she'd witnessed as a Catholic nun.

I ripped the sheet from the pole, quickly looking around to make sure no one had seen me, and stuffed it in my pocket. How could this nun betray her sisters and give such a talk? Surely she was lying. The nuns who taught me had been strict. But they weren't what this paper implied—wicked, evil, or strange.

At the Academy, I found Lester in the basement near the boiler. He looked up and smiled when he saw me.

"Just in time," he said. "I was wondering if you were sick." He turned back to a cabinet and pulled out paintbrushes and rags. An older man, he had the short, stocky build of a prize-fighter. His face was fleshy and full of deep creases, and he was the only man I'd ever describe as having eyes that sparkled.

"Sorry," I mumbled.

He turned quickly at the sound of my gloomy voice. "You sure you're not sick?"

"I'm fine," I protested. But my irritation betrayed me. I didn't want to—in fact, I couldn't—tell him about Adam. So I pulled the paper from my pocket. "Who is this? You ever hear of her?"

Lester took the page from my hand and read it, scratching his head as he did so. His smile left him and he frowned once or twice. When he was done, he ripped the paper in two and fed it into the furnace, clanging the door shut with a loud bang.

"Did you notice any other ones around the school?" he asked.

"I didn't look."

"When we're done painting, we'll go out and see. Get them down before any of the sisters find them." He muttered a curse under his breath, something about people whose names I didn't recognize.

As we walked up to the office to be painted, I pressed Lester for more information. "Why would a nun do that sort of thing—give talks like that?" I wanted him to tell me she was a charlatan, but I didn't want to ask outright. I was always afraid of something—in this case, disappointment.

Lester stopped on a first floor landing and jabbed his finger at my chest. "You don't believe that crap, do you? That Sister Lucretia is no more an ex-nun than I'm an ex-pope. She's a crazy woman. Was in an insane asylum." He lowered his voice when a student came onto the landing and scurried upstairs. "The local Klan probably invited her here to get people all riled up before the vote."

He led the way upstairs but didn't say any more. When we reached the empty office, he spread cloths over the desk, opened the window, laid out the brushes, and began mixing the paint—all in quick succession. He told me to put my jacket and cap where they wouldn't get stained, and gave me an old, oversized shirt to protect my other clothes.

Then we started painting. While we worked, I got him talking about the vote coming up, something Lester called "the School Question." Oregonians, he said, were being asked to put the Academy and schools like it out of business by voting on whether children should be required to go to public schools only. Some people, Lester said, believed Catholics were a threat to the country, and all the more dangerous when educated in Catholic schools.

"They want to take people like you and me and put us on a boat back home," he seethed, swiping neat strokes of cream-colored paint on the wall.

Back home? At first, I thought of Baltimore, and marveled at how anything good could come from such hate. Then I realized what he meant. Matuski was my last name, and to the people behind the School Question, any boat they put me on would be headed to Poland, a land as familiar to me as the moon.

"I'm an American," I said to Lester, sounding as incredulous as I felt. "Born and raised here."

He let out a bitter laugh. "To them, you're a Bolshevik plotter, son. All of us are, even the good sisters who run this school." He gently waved the paintbrush in the air. "*Mongrels*, they call us."

It was crazy enough to be laughable. My name, Matuski, might sound foreign, but Lester's name was Grenton. Sure, it was shortened by some relative he'd never known, but Lester's parents were born here in America, and so was he. To think of someone like Lester as a "mongrel" and not a true American was beyond comprehension. Nobody would fall for those lies, I thought. They were too outrageous.

After a while, Lester turned and smiled at me. "Don't you worry about it, son. The sisters have been talking to some people. They'll make sure the school stays open, no matter what."

I had to confess, I didn't really care that much what happened to the school, except I did need the money it paid me. But I didn't like people thinking poorly of folks like Lester and me just because we were Catholics with foreign-sounding last names. And it seemed wildly unfair to have a deranged lunatic spreading lies about the good sisters just because a bunch of hateful people had a crazy idea about schools that no one in their right mind would be inclined to support.

After we cleaned up, I helped Lester scour the neighborhood for more posted notices advertising "Sister Lucretia's" talk. We found a good half dozen, and he suggested looking for, and removing, their possible replacements the next day.

By the time I headed home, I realized I'd spent the entire day thinking about this School Question nonsense, and not one second thinking about Adam. I guess every cloud does have a silver lining after all.

———◦•✦•◦———

I stopped at home before going to meet Gus for my paycheck. As I'd guessed, Adam hadn't been aware of my absence, and Pete was nowhere to be seen.

After I softly closed the front door, I heard movement upstairs and took the steps two at a time to remind Adam to stay away from the windows, in case Miller was sniffing around.

"I'm hungry," Adam said. "Does Pete have any eggs?" He stood in the doorway to the room we shared on the second floor.

"Don't hang around the kitchen, Adam," I warned. "Miller can see right through the window." Miller might be searching for Adam elsewhere, but there was no reason for Adam to get careless.

"I gotta eat something. I'm going to be on the run soon." He scratched his head and stared at me. For the first time, he looked tired, with dark circles under his eyes and a day-old beard shadowing his chin. It made me think to rub my own jaw, where there was only a fine peach-fuzz of growth. I didn't need to shave half as much as Adam.

"Go shave," I told Adam. "You look like a bum. I'll bring you back some food after I meet Gus."

Without responding, he turned toward the bathroom. I left, feeling troubled and tired. I realized this was the way you felt when you had responsibilities. It was probably the way Adam had felt when he'd taken care of me.

I squared my shoulders. I was up to the task.

Chapter Four

Pete's place was on the edge of downtown on a short street of houses that had seen better days. Once a bright yellow, it now had a spotted look, with wooden clapboards showing through the paint. The owner next door had wisely painted his home brown so its peeling paint blended in with the wood underneath. Most neighbors' front yards were tiny and weed-filled, overridden with crabgrass and dandelion roots. The homes were all close to the busy road, which filled with cars and horse-drawn wagons on their way into town every morning. Portland still had a lot of horses—unlike Baltimore, where automobiles greatly outnumbered horse-drawn vehicles, creating a daily parade of fancy new machines.

All the houses in Pete's neighborhood were alike in style and size, with porches running the width of the homes. During summers, folks lounged about on their porches, catching the cool river breezes and talking to each other. The first summer we were there, Pete introduced us to his neighbors, taking us from porch to porch. There wasn't a single boy my age—just older folks and small children. In Baltimore, I had my friends from school and a half dozen other kids from the neighborhood. We played stickball in the alley and did pranks on a dare. Adam smoothed over more than one scrape for me, apologizing to a neighbor when Billy and

I had tipped over a trash bin, and not telling Ma when I played hooky from school to watch Julian pitch in a baseball game in Patterson Park.

I've never made friends like that in Portland. I wasn't in school long enough to break into the ring of buddies already formed, and working took a toll on how much time I had left for even thinking about fun. Besides, there was no point in getting close to anybody when Adam and I were planning to head back to where my real friends lived.

When Pete showed us around those first months, though, he lingered a bit at the Petrovich household, where a young widow was raising twin daughters, both about nine years old. Sometimes, Pete stopped there after work, which led me to think he was courting Mrs. Petrovich.

A few blocks over from the Petrovich house was the Jasluzek store. It reminded me of home, of the store where Ma had worked. Smelling of cheese and coffee, it had broad planked flooring and shelves of foodstuffs with exotic brand names on the labels. Standing behind the counter in his dirty apron, Mr. Jasluzek always smiled when you came through the door. He saw every visitor as a potential bearer of good news, or at the very least, as a purchaser, which was always good news to him. With bushy black hair and a thick, neat moustache, Jasluzek carried himself as straight and proud as a town mayor.

Jasluzek's store always evoked in me an odd mixture of con-tentment and sadness. I'd breathe deep the heady aroma of all that food, close my eyes, and feel back at home—back to a time when I'd stop in the store where Ma worked and she'd slip me a krushiki or peppermint stick, some small treat accompanied by a secret smile. I didn't worry about anything back then. Not about my next meal. Not about my mother. And certainly not about Adam.

But when I opened my eyes, the reality of the present day

would crash in on me as quickly as the returning tide, the ache deeper because of the good memories from home. It was a double-edged sword, Jasluzek's store.

That afternoon at the store, I figured I'd pick up my papers and pay from Gus, and then head right back to hand the money over to Adam before I began my route. Wouldn't you know it, though? Today, Gus Winston had other plans.

A short fat man with wavy brown hair that crept down his forehead, Gus was always grinning. But his smile and his friendliness hid a vicious anger. More than once, Gus, without losing the smile, had berated me in the foulest language for not selling my extra papers. Gus gave his paperboys a half-dozen more papers than their routes required. We were expected to sell the extras by standing on street corners and yelling at passers-by to buy them. I hated that part of the job, but if I didn't sell the papers, Gus would take the money for them out of my pay. I thought Gus treated me worse than the other boys, but I was glad for the job and just shrugged off the "special treatment."

As I cut the wire binding on my bundle of papers, I looked hopefully at Gus, who reached into the pocket of his dapper flannel trousers. Gus was a good dresser, with new, sharply creased pants and turned-up cuffs, clean shirts with soft collars, and a hat that went well with everything he wore. Today it was a rounded, soft brown derby that matched his tweedy double-breasted jacket. Straightening, I waited for him to hand over my money, but was disappointed when he pulled out a slip of paper instead.

"Here," he said, handing it to me. "I've got a treat for you boys today." Smiling like someone with a secret, he rocked on his heels, waiting for me to open the folded paper.

Printed inside was an address. Looking up at Gus, confused, I inwardly cursed. I didn't have time for puzzles. Adam would be waiting.

"What's this?" I asked.

"It's the address of the *Telegram* office, boy! I've arranged a tour for all of you—of a big city newsroom! Wait 'til you see it. It'll put a spring in your step as you do your route. You'll see what this grand enterprise is all about!" He pointed to the newspapers, the product of the "grand enterprise" he was so proud of. Headlines blared out election news, especially about the school vote coming up. I'd pay more attention to that now.

On any other day, the prospect of visiting the newsroom of one of the city's biggest newspapers would have filled me with excitement. But today, all I could think about was keeping my brother out of harm's way. I needed to give him my pay as soon as possible.

Swallowing hard, I looked at Gus and waited for him to hand over my money. But he just stood there, beaming like a well-groomed Santa Claus on Christmas Day, his hands in his pockets and his face pinking up from excitement.

"Gus," I said, "can I have my pay now?"

Laughing, he shook his head. "That's part of the treat. You're going to meet the publisher of the paper, and he'll be handing you your pay today. It'll be a great honor. Aren't you excited?"

Thinking of Adam waiting for me, I wanted to say, "No, I'm not excited." But I nodded and thanked Gus, promising to meet him at the newsroom entrance.

Once I left, my first thought was to rush home and tell Adam I wasn't going to get the money until much later. But as I walked away from the store, I caught sight of a police officer. Standing straight and proud in his blue uniform, Officer John Miller looked right at me from under the brim of his cap. He didn't say a word, but I got the message—he was watching me. If I did anything unusual, like heading home before completing my newspaper route, he'd be on me quicker than a fly on honey. *Crap!* More than once, I'd thought of giving up this delivery route and looking for other work. Now I wished I'd done it. I was too old for this anyway. Let the young pups take over.

I raced through my paper route, the neighborhood near Pete's house, that afternoon. I hurled papers onto porches and lawns with hardly a thought as to where they landed. Once, I nearly hit an old grandma, managing to catch myself right before tossing it toward her as she left her home. But I was distracted by Miller, who kept turning up at the end of every block. He even waved to me once and said a few words.

"Working hard, Vladimir?" he asked, with sugar-coated poison in his voice.

I didn't answer him but went on my way. He followed, ambling a few steps behind.

"Started to convert your newspaper friends yet, Vlad?"

Still I said nothing.

"What's that? You don't understand the language, Trotsky?"

"My name's Carl," I spat back at him.

"Oh yes. Karl, like that fellow Marx who started all that trouble over in Russia we're dealing with now."

Placing his hands on his hips, he stepped in front of me, forcing me to brush his elbow as I passed. He immediately dusted off the spot. "Your brother certainly took Karl Marx's lessons to heart—stealing from the wealthy Petersons what he wanted for himself. The Petersons are nice folks—good Americans, too."

My face reddened with anger and my hands balled into fists again. *Damn him!* He wasn't worth a word. But still I couldn't hold back—not after seeing that stupid Sister Lucretia advertisement, and after hearing Lester's story about the school vote. Who the hell did Miller think he was? Did he have more claim to being here than I did? Than Adam did?

Without looking at him, I grumbled out loud, "He didn't do nothing wrong. There are lots of other folks who could have taken that stuff." But my voice sounded thin with rage, not at all like the robust retort I'd imagined when I'd heard it in my mind.

I would have kept going but I heard him laughing behind me, a slow chuckle that told me he thought I was crazy for believing my brother was innocent.

Whirling around to face him, I shifted my webbed paper carrier higher on my aching shoulder.

"You're just too lazy to find the real thief," I said, looking him in the eye. Now my voice was stronger. Strong and low.

His smile dropped from his face as he stared hard at me for a few seconds. Let him try to beat me. He'd have to catch me first.

"If I had good evidence someone else did it, I'd follow it in a minute," he said, reaching over and snapping his finger next to my ear in an explosive pop. But I wouldn't give him the satisfaction of seeing me cringe or rub my ear. I stood tall and still. It felt good . . . but scary, too.

"Why do you care about this stupid burglary anyway?" I asked. "Don't you have murderers to catch?" My feet were planted solidly on the concrete pavement. I gritted my teeth, waiting for Miller to box my ears or smack me for being "uppity."

Instead, his mood changed and he sighed so heavily his shoulders sank several inches. "You think this is a stupid burglary, son? Let me ask you something—is your mother alive?"

My eyes widened. "She passed on last year," I answered. Why had he asked this question? What else did he know?

"She give you anything special before she died?"

Without answering, I glanced over his shoulder, thinking

of the rosary the priest had given Adam and he had given me. It never left my pocket. I could feel it there even as I stared at Officer Miller. It was part religious token, part good luck charm, and mostly a piece of family memory. Ma had given Adam our father's pocket watch. I knew he kept it gleaming and never went anywhere without it.

Officer Miller continued in a deep, quiet voice, "Well, if she did, then you'd know how special those things are. The jewelry stolen from the Petersons was just like that—a gift from their grandmother before she passed away. Mrs. Peterson is in despair over the loss. It was the only thing she had from her mother, because the rest of her mother's possessions had been destroyed in a fire the year before."

Now my face warmed, and I couldn't look at him. I didn't want him to be right about anything, even something as simple as the Petersons. It was easier to think they deserved their loss, no matter who was responsible for it. It was easier to think they wouldn't miss a few pieces of jewelry when they had so much. It was easier to think only of Adam's plight and not their pain. I continued to stare past him at the horizon and didn't move.

"Son, I know you love your brother," Miller said.

Still not looking at him, I shifted my weight from one foot to the next. If I didn't hurry, I'd be late meeting Gus and the others and I'd never get my pay. It was better to think of practical things like that instead of the more complicated feelings now wrapped around the Peterson theft.

"But wrong is wrong," he said. "And no amount of brotherly love makes it right." He paused, then the corner of his mouth lifted into something between a smile and a sneer. "Be on your way, Mr. Marx. But I'll be watching you."

I waited for him to pass by me down the street, then I sped up to finish my route in record time. As I came to the last home,

I immediately started hawking the remaining papers. A jumble of feelings churned up inside, bubbling into a bold effort as I shouted "Paper! Evening Paper!" louder and stronger than I ever had in the past. I was shouting out everything I felt—confusion, fear, sadness—my voice echoing off walls and bouncing back two-fold. I sold those newspapers in ten minutes. I'd never done it faster.

Finally, I could go. I debated whether to hurry home and tell Adam about the delay. But I was afraid if I did, Miller would follow me and I'd miss the opportunity to get my cash, which was really what my brother needed most of all. I'd focus on that and sort out the rest of my feelings later.

Chapter Five

The *Telegram* office was on Washington Street, in a big new building with a clock tower looming over its corner entrance like a watchful eye peering into your soul. Not wanting to spring for a trolley fare, I walked and ran the few miles to the building. Out of breath and tired, I arrived at the front doorway just before the appointed hour. About a dozen other boys were waiting. Some were just young kids who knew each other from school and talked about baseball, but many were like me, in long pants, quiet and keeping to themselves, their hands clutched one over the other on the empty webbing of their newspaper carriers. Gus arrived a few seconds later, approaching the door like the ringmaster in a circus act.

"Come in, come in," he said, waving his hands toward the door.

As we shuffled into the lobby, I looked up at the clock. It was nearly four. Adam had expected me home about an hour ago. How long would Gus's tour take? I needed to get out of there before Adam started looking for me or before Pete came home. Pete knew Adam was in trouble and had argued with him about it, telling him to "act like a man" and other things that knifed me to hear them. Would Pete go so far as to give Adam up to the police? I wasn't sure, but I couldn't take the chance.

Inside the lobby, a few men in bowler hats and derbies stood patiently in line at a cashier's window. Behind a metal grille, a young man with slickly combed brown hair, tweed suit, starched collar, and bowtie stamped papers and looked busy. Otherwise, the area was empty. Gus led us to the elevators, and we all managed to squeeze into one.

The elevator sped us up to the third floor. When the doors opened, I was surprised to see a huge open room filled with desks and tables. I'd always figured something as important as a newspaper would have offices fit for a king, with a separate room for each reporter. But this wasn't an office at all. It was more like one giant hall—a gymnasium filled with desks, covered with typewriters and piles of papers. The floors were littered with crumpled balls of all kinds of paper—lined notebook pages, typing paper, carbons, even newspapers. The air smelled dusty and stale, overlaid with a strong whiff of ink.

But there were no people. That the room was empty didn't seem to surprise or disappoint Gus. Still acting like a ringmaster of some sort, he shepherded us to a glass-enclosed office at the far end of the room.

"Where is everybody?" I heard a small kid whisper. "They gonna tell us the paper's shutting down?"

Turning around and walking backwards, Gus explained, "On an evening paper, the reporters work early morning shifts. They're done for the day."

They were done for the day, all right—all but one fellow who looked like a kid kept after school. I noticed him as we neared the office. Tall and skinny, he tapped away at a typewriter near the windows, a cigar hanging out the corner of his mouth. He had thin brown hair and pasty skin, and he didn't bother to look up as we trooped by. His jacket and hat hung on a wooden hook by his desk. The clothes looked expensive—the hat was soft black felt, and the jacket was some new cut with a yoked back. I'd seen one in a department store window downtown. The phone on his desk rang and he picked it up.

"Briggs," he said in a voice that sounded like gravel. "Yeah, you said you were at the church bazaar the night of the murder, but I got a source says they saw you coming out of Blarney's speakeasy two blocks from where the man was shot."

We were delayed while Gus went into the office to see if the publisher was ready, so I wound up listening as Briggs peppered the caller with questions that fit a police detective better than a newspaper man.

A police detective. The hair on my neck stood up. Briggs was chasing down a story just the way the cops chased down a suspect. But Briggs didn't seem content with easy answers. He was digging for more.

A few seconds later, Gus introduced us to the publisher in the glass-enclosed office, but I kept looking over at Briggs's desk. After typing for a few moments, he stopped and looked at what he'd written. Scowling, he reached for his phone. I heard him say, "Briggs here from the *Telegram*. Is Officer Reeves around?" And then he asked the officer questions in that very same tough tone of voice. He was treating the officer just the way he'd treated the suspect—with a heavy dose of cynicism. He didn't take anything for granted, didn't believe someone just because he had a title or wore a uniform.

Or had a good American-sounding name.

As the publisher spoke about how important we all were to "the Fourth Estate," I kept glancing at Briggs, who was off the phone now. After pecking away on his typewriter for a few seconds, he leaned back and crossed his arms over his chest, as if unhappy with what he'd just written. His hand hovered over his phone, but he pulled it back, stuck his cigar in the corner of his mouth, and resumed typing.

An idea began to form in my mind. The police weren't the only ones who investigated crimes. Reporters like Briggs did, too. In fact, Briggs questioned both suspects *and* the police. He got the full picture—not just the one the police wanted to look at. Adam had said I was smart, and I was smart enough to know when I needed help from someone who knew how to investigate things.

As we received our pay and a little tin pin stamped with the newspaper's name, I kept my eye on Briggs, awestruck by his determination and energy. After typing furiously for a while, he pulled his paper from the carriage and read it, a smile spreading across his face. Then he headed for a desk at the other end of the newsroom, where he dropped his paper into a wooden bin.

Maybe I could talk to him before we left. Maybe I could ask him to help me investigate the Peterson burglary case and get Adam off the hook. *Maybe, maybe, maybe.*

"Any questions?" The publisher, a tall man with white hair and a squarish face, looked around the room at all of us newsboys. Nobody said anything. My guess was they were as eager to leave as I was. But just when it looked like we'd be dismissed, Briggs began moving. He was leaving! His coat over his shoulders, the cigar in his left hand, he was taking such quick strides toward the elevators that I was sure he'd be gone in a few seconds.

"I have a question!" I piped up, my head turning back toward the publisher. Gus beamed at me, probably proud that I wanted to learn more. "Who was that?" I pointed in the direction the reporter had gone.

The publisher smiled. "That was Vincent G. Briggs, our ace reporter."

Vincent G. Briggs—I repeated the full name to myself, afraid I'd forget it. I might not be able to talk to him now, but I'd call him later. Yeah, that might be better anyway. I wouldn't have to give him my name. I could just give him a "tip"—*You know that Peterson burglary?* I heard myself saying. *Well, they're after the wrong fellow for it.*

———◆◆◆———

When I got home, Pete was rattling pans in the kitchen and preparing to make us something for dinner. Usually he just fried up some sausage or scrambled some eggs. Pete wasn't much of a chef, and when he found out we didn't much care for his cooking, he stopped trying. Most nights, we fended for ourselves, making sandwiches or eating cheese and cold leftover potatoes.

"That you, *syneczku?*" he called when he heard the door creak open. Like Ma had, Pete still spoke with a Polish accent, and occasionally sprinkled in some Polish words with his English. I cringed, not because of his use of Polish, but because the words he used were more appropriate for a small boy.

"Yeah, it's me!" I threw my newspaper carrier in a corner by the front door and took a look upstairs. "Adam?" I whispered. Nothing but silence greeted me. Where had he gone? Would Pete know? Had Pete come home from his milk route, found Adam, and immediately taken him by the scruff of his neck to the police station to face his problem "like a man"?

I ran upstairs and searched each of the three small rooms. No Adam. His clothes were gone, too. Racing back, I veered through the living room and beyond, to the back of the house and the kitchen.

Pete stood at the stove, pushing a thin pork chop around in a frying pan. About six feet tall, Pete was all bones and no muscle. While most preferred the "toothbrush" moustache now, Pete sported a bushy one that drooped over the edges of his thin mouth, making him look sad and droopy. Today, his long, horse-like face was unshaven, and his dark brown hair looked like it needed washing. When he heard me, he turned.

"Didn't know where you were, so I only made one of these," he said, pointing with his fork to the pork chop. Looking at the meat and then at me, he said, "You can share it, if you want." But from the regret in his voice, it was clear he was hungry. Hungry, but not angry. Adam must have fled before Pete came home and discovered him hiding out.

"No, thanks. I'll just have some milk."

"There's some hard-boiled eggs," Pete said as I walked to the ice box. Yawning, he turned the pork chop over. It sizzled in the pan. "Did you make them?"

No, I hadn't, but Adam must have. "Yup," I said, pulling out the milk bottle. The rich cream was already gone from the top. Somebody had drunk it already. Where had Adam gone?

"How'd you find time with your jobs?" Pete asked. He rarely asked me about my activities, so I knew he was trying to find out more.

"Uh, I boiled 'em before I went to the Academy this morning," I said. I poured myself a big glass of milk and grabbed a piece of bread from the white table.

"That's strange," Pete said, "They were still warm when I came home about a half hour ago."

I didn't say anything. I sat at the table, drank my milk, and ate my bread. Pete's pork chop sure smelled good, and I was mighty hungry after running around so much. I was tired, too. I'd been up before dawn and hadn't had a chance to nap—as Adam had done. Now the fatigue of the day caught up with me, weighting me to the table as if a stone had fallen across my shoulders. My eyelids already felt heavy, and I wanted nothing more than to go to sleep. Pete came over to the table with the frying pan and placed it in the corner. Then he grabbed two plates, two forks, and two knives from a cabinet above the sink and a drawer beside it, and put one set in front of me.

"You look like you need something hot," he said. Cutting the pork chop in two, he gave me a piece before sitting down.

"Thanks," I said, not looking at him. Grabbing a fork, I dove in. It tasted good and I sopped up the juice from my plate with some of the bread. We ate in silence. Pete was busy reading some pamphlet, and it was making him angry. Every once in a while, he cursed under his breath and shook his head. "Lies, all lies," he muttered at one point. "I cannot believe anybody believes this nonsense! Not in this country."

I could only see a little of the pamphlet. It looked like a story called *The Old Cedar School*. When Pete saw my interest, he slid it toward me and I started to read.

It *was* a story, all right, but what a strange and ugly tale it was. It was more of the Sister Lucretia falsehoods, a fantastic story of a pioneer who helped build his town's school. But his children grew up and sent their own kids to other schools, including a Catholic one like the Academy where I worked.

But in *The Old Cedar School*, the Catholic school was called the "Academy of St. Gregory's Holy Toe Nail," where students learned stuff like "histomorphology, the Petrine Supremacy, Transubstantiation, and the beatification of Saint Caviar."

It was a crazy tale, and I laughed reading it, but Pete's face was grim. Before long, I found out why—and my stomach turned. The author described a "Roman Catholic Bishop runnin' out from the fir grove toward the school house, a wearin' a long black robe an' a manicurist's lace shirt." The bishop in the story helped burn down the public school, which the author described as "the last torch of liberty."

I couldn't help myself—I cursed, and for once, Pete didn't

scold me. "No bishop burnt down a school," I said. "I would have heard about that if it happened."

Pete frowned. "*Nie*," he said in Polish. *No.*

"Who wrote this story?" I asked, thinking it was probably the same folks who let a madwoman give speeches about nuns.

Pete pushed his plate away and leaned into the table, his hands together in front of him. "It's always the way." He stared beyond me as he spoke. "It's because people like to blame bad things on people who are not like them."

Blaming bad things on people who are different? Through the fog of my fatigue, an idea emerged. "That's probably why the cops are after Adam," I said, unable to keep the bitterness out of my voice. I knew Miller didn't like Poles, but maybe this whole school business was fanning the flames, making Adam's bad luck even worse.

"You're a good boy, Carl," Pete said slowly, as if searching for the right words, "and I know it has not been easy when *twoja mamusia*—your mother—was lost to us . . ."

I looked at my plate and gritted my teeth. Pete was working up to something—something I didn't want to hear. My breath came fast and blood pumped hard in my ears.

"Adam's had it hard, too," he said.

"Adam's a *dobry czlowiek* (a good person) and you know it," I insisted, using the Polish that Pete was comfortable with. I knew exactly what Uncle Pete was trying to tell me—that if Adam was in trouble, it was because things had been so topsy-turvy in our lives after our mother died.

Pete sat up straight. "If Adam's done something wrong, it's not because he's a Catholic or the son of Poles. Don't ever forget that."

He scraped his chair back and took his plate to the sink. Then he headed for the stairs. "I'm very tired," he said. "I'm going to lie down. Wash up those dishes, please."

◆•✦•◆

Adam's disappearance caused several problems for me. First, not knowing where he was worried me to death. I didn't trust him to be as careful as I was, and I kept imagining him turning a corner and running straight into Miller's arms.

But I had another problem—what to do with my check. If Adam didn't show up before the morning, Pete might ask me where it was, and I'd have to give it to him if there was a bill to pay. In fact, when he needed the cash, Pete usually asked for it as soon as I came home on paydays. Maybe he didn't need it, or maybe he'd been too tired, or too distracted by that stupid *Cedar School* story, to ask.

I was tired, too, and after cleaning up the kitchen, I went up to my room and fell asleep with my clothes still on. I'd only meant to close my eyes for a little while, but when I woke up, it was pitch black. Night had fallen. Rubbing my eyes, I wondered what time it was.

From down the hall, I heard a soft *click-click*, followed by a hiss.

In a flash, I was standing, my eyes darting this way and that, wondering what to do. I heard it again—this time a barrage of clicks and then the hiss. It was coming from the back of the house. Walking to the doorway, I considered waking up Pete, but then my sleepy brain focused on the sound and I figured it out. Someone was throwing pebbles at the back window.

Click, click, click, the stones sounded. Then, "Pssst!"

It was Adam!

In my stocking feet, I ran to the empty back room and pushed up the heavy sash. As soon as the cold night air hit my face, I heard his voice.

"Took you long enough!" he said from below. "Open up the door. I don't have my key."

I practically flew downstairs and let him in the back door.

"Look, I can't stay," he said, his voice hushed but nervous, a far cry from the cavalier attitude he'd shown the day before. "Miller came by yesterday when you weren't here. He was banging on the door something fierce. I had to hide in the furnace room."

"In the coal bin?"

"No," he laughed, looking at me like I was crazy to suggest it again. "I just stayed away from the windows. I was in the furnace room an hour until I was sure he'd left. Then I figured I'd better be on my way before Pete came home because I knew Miller would be back. I took some eggs."

"I know," I said.

"Where were you? Did you get the money?"

I explained how Gus had set up a tour of the newsroom and how I'd run into Miller myself on my paper route. Then I fished my paycheck out of my pocket and handed it over.

"You gotta cash it," he said, handing it back. "I thought that's what you were going to do."

"Didn't have time. I was hurrying to get home." And then, of course, I'd fallen asleep. I'd failed him. We stood awkwardly in the shadows of the kitchen, and I had the sense Adam was waiting for me to come up with an alternative plan.

"You can hide out here tonight, and I'll cash it for you in the morning."

"No, Pete'll ask you for it. Probably even wake you up before he heads out."

He was right. The rent was coming due. Pete was always short when the rent was due.

"I'll . . . I'll tell him I lost it!" I whispered. "I was going to tell him that anyway."

"He'll just tell you to get another one, and get them to stop payment on the first check. No, you've got to tell him you cashed it. Spent it on the way home."

"On what?"

"The movies, a craps game, a gift for a girl—I dunno." He sounded frustrated with me, but I knew he was tired and let it go. "Pete'll beat the crap out of you."

"That's not what I'm worried about. I'm worried about coming up with a story he'll believe." I wondered what time it was. I was still sleepy and not thinking straight. "Look, you're going to have to keep hiding until tomorrow. Where'd you go before?"

"Nowhere special."

"Pete won't check on us before he heads out," I said. "Go upstairs and lie down."

As Adam breezed by, I smelled something on his breath that made my blood run cold.

It was the woody odor of whiskey.

Chapter Six

Adam reeked of the stuff. He must have been drinking all night. Prohibition had made booze illegal. Was he trying to get in trouble?

The liquor on my brother's breath that night sparked a change in my outlook. It wasn't the drinking that bothered me so much. It was the sense that he wasn't trying anymore. For as long as I could remember, Adam had always been the optimist, showing me in word and deed that things could and would get better—that the next day could exceed the promise of the last. But now he seemed to be daring the world to strike him down, gambling with both our futures.

I had selfishly relied on his good disposition to see me through my own blue moods, I realized. Not for one second had I thought how hard, and tiring, it must have been always pushing me along the path of life. I was already tired—and I'd only been the problem-solver for a short time now. He had to have been worn down. I hoped to God it wasn't too late for me to make it up to him—to at least give him some of the support he'd given me.

Even so, I was scared I would fail. Maybe I was too "scrawny" to keep him on firmer ground. I needed another Adam to help me save him—not even Vincent G. Briggs would be enough. I was a smart one, Adam had said, but I didn't know if I was the right kind of smart—the way an animal is smart, sensing danger in the air from miles away.

An unease settled over me, making my skin prickly and my breath fast. I found myself wishing I could hurry everything along so I could tell if something would thwart my plans and I could adjust accordingly. I wished I could snap my fingers and have this "ace reporter" start making phone calls and talking big, like I'd heard him talking the day before, to solve my brother's case. I wished I could keep Adam out of more trouble. I wished I felt as confident as I had in that newsroom. I wished Adam and I could start planning our move back East.

Adam breathed easily in the bed across from me, sleeping the sleep of the untroubled. I was awake so long I heard Pete get up before dawn to head into work. For one heart-stopping moment, it sounded like he was going to open the door to our room and check on us. As I heard him walk down the hall and pause before our door, I got ready to spring out of bed and stall him. But his shadow passed and eventually I heard him downstairs, turning on the spigot and making himself some coffee. I realized, exhaling, that he wouldn't ask for my pay and he wouldn't find Adam. We were lucky.

Once I was sure he was out of the house, I arose and washed up. I had a lot to do today. I needed to stop by the Academy to see if Lester had any work for me, I had to cash that check and get the money back to Adam, and I had to contact Vincent Briggs.

The first job was simple enough. I headed to the Academy without even grabbing a bite to eat. The day was cooler and grayer than the day before, and I turned up the collar of my jacket against the chill, thrusting my hands into my pockets.

When I got to the Academy, Lester was touching up the paint job we'd finished yesterday. He said he didn't have anything more for me, a relief since I had other things I had to do.

"You could check around for those announcements, though," he said as he stood on a ladder by the window.

"What announcements?"

He turned and smiled. "The lying woman who calls herself an ex-nun."

I'd forgotten about "Sister Lucretia" and the School Question. One trouble had replaced another so quickly I couldn't keep them all straight. I'd not even looked at telephone poles during my walk to work.

Lester pointed to a pile of papers on the sill. "I found a bunch on my way in."

"Aw, geez, Lester, nobody believes that stuff." I was too busy to care about outrageous garbage like that.

"It would be a great help if you could look around for them," he said. "A bunch of us are taking different sections of the city."

"I . . . I can't today. Have to do some things," I mumbled.

I nodded and headed for the hallway, nearly running into a real sister. She looked startled but quickly stepped out of the way, signaling to a line of uniformed girls to follow her. The girls were of various ages but had one thing in common—all were as thin as rails, and scared-looking. I knew at least some were orphans. You'd have to have a heart of steel not to feel sorry for them—I had my own motherless sorrow to prick those feelings to life. Out of respect, I pulled off my cap, and I watched them pass, the short black-robed nun at the lead coaxing them with kind words. Her voice was accented, and I remembered Lester telling me once that these nuns—the Sisters of the Holy Names of Jesus and Mary— were originally from Montreal. Many of them spoke French. A few were recruited right here in Portland.

After the line passed me, I slid out the back door and headed toward my neighborhood. I spotted a few of the nasty posters and removed them, cramming two or three into my pocket. I felt bad for turning Lester down when he asked for help, so I'd try to remember to keep an eye out for the posters in the days ahead.

My next stop was the Jasluzek store, where I'd cash my check from Gus. I rushed there as soon as he opened and asked him if he'd do me a favor and save me a trip to the bank.

"Sure, son," he said, eyeing me suspiciously as he opened his cash drawer. "Just sign it over first." While he counted out the amount, he glanced up at me over the top of the embossed register. Would he ask why I needed the money so fast? I didn't wait to find out. As soon as he handed me the bills and change, I thanked him and ran off.

Luckily for me, Miller must have had the day off—I didn't see him at all. Cash in hand, I raced back home, handing over the cash to Adam, at last feeling that I'd actually solved a problem. He sat at the kitchen table eating some of those hardboiled eggs he'd cooked the day before. He looked dirty and sick, and I thought about talking to him about avoiding speakeasies, about how everything would be all right as soon as I got Vincent Briggs on the case.

If I was to step into the role of leader, I had to learn how to say those things—how to prop people up when they were feeling low.

I even thought of saying what Pete had said to me—that being Catholic and Polish didn't make you bad and it was unfair of folks to think so. But as the words formed in my head, they sounded childish, unconnected to the reality at hand, and I became afraid he'd laugh at me if I tried to give him advice. Why should Adam listen to me when I didn't know half of what the world had to offer or deny you? After all, I'd always leaned on him for advice, for cheer, for a map of life itself. Instead of a speech, now I just wanted to say I was sorry.

But I said nothing.

I heated up some coffee for us both, and eventually talked to Adam a little bit about where he might be able to stay—if the sawmill wasn't a good place, I could scout out some abandoned homes. It was a one-sided conversation. He didn't say much, and when he was finished eating and drinking, he washed up his dishes and headed upstairs without a word. In a few minutes, he returned, standing in the doorway to the kitchen while I, still at the table, stared into the distance.

Light streamed through the front windows of the bungalow, silhouetting his figure before me. He'd combed his hair and changed his clothes, and he carried his belongings in a tidy bundle by his side.

I remembered him looking exactly like that in the Chicago train station when we'd made our way west. I'd been sitting on a bench then, while he'd gone off to find out what train we needed to get on next. I'd waited a long time—so long I'd been afraid he'd lost me. My face had begun to burn with unshed tears as panic crawled up my throat. And then, out of the throng of dark-suited men and black-dressed women, he appeared, standing before me as he stood now, confident and serious.

"I'm heading to the station," he now said quietly.

"What?"

"I have to get out of here, Carl. You know that."

Get out of here? I hadn't thought he'd actually leave town without me. I'd thought he'd hide away somewhere in Portland, in a different neighborhood, until we cleared his name and could leave together.

"But we were both going to go home," I said. "I just need more money. I need—"

He shook his head. A smile played on his face. "You need a better brother is what you need."

"Adam, you'll get better—"

He cut me off with a sharp laugh. "See what I mean? You agree."

"No, that's not what I meant. I meant *things'll* get better. You'll see."

"I can't wait, Carl." He looked down. "You'll do all right without me. You're doing fine now."

A thousand thoughts tightened around my throat and chest. They squeezed the happiness out of me, leaving only a vacuum. It didn't matter what he said. I still counted on him. How could I make it home alone? Anger tripped over sadness and I was afraid, for a fleeting second, that I might cry, just one more sign I wasn't ready to be on my own. Too often I felt and acted like a kid.

I studied his face, feeling like I had to memorize it. When would I ever see him again? My heart racing, I stood and came around to him.

"How will I get in touch with you?" I asked.

"I'll send you a letter or something," he said, walking toward the front door.

"Real soon," I insisted, walking after him. "Or call the Jasluzek store. He'll get a message to me."

"When I can, I will."

"You can tell me where you've gone. I can join you." If I kept talking, maybe he would stay.

At the front door, he stopped and shrugged a little, which meant he didn't want to let me down, but he couldn't say what I wanted to hear. I held out my hand like a gentleman might do. A smile pushed up the corners of his mouth as he gripped my hand tight and shook it.

"Take care of yourself," he said, his voice unnaturally bright. Touching his cap, he turned and left.

I watched him run down the street, glancing behind him when he thought he'd heard someone. His head turned and his eyes caught my gaze. A broad smile lit his face and he waved, as if he were heading off to work or school. My throat burned and I bit my lip. "He's not going away forever," I whispered to myself. I'd fix it so he could return. I'd fix it so we could both go home together—just as we'd planned. I'd clear his name, then he'd come back, and we could start our journey together. Baltimore was where we'd both been happy. It's where we'd played in alleys together. Where we'd gone to school and shared stories before falling asleep. Where we'd had a mother who loved us. Maybe if I could get him back there, he'd be the same brother I used to know.

Action was what I needed. When his figure disappeared around a corner, I grabbed my own jacket and cap and hurried downtown. Retracing my steps from the day before, I managed to find the employee entrance to the big *Telegram* newspaper building. A man in a dark suit, sitting behind a desk by the elevators, asked me what "business" I had there today.

Before I could think enough to be fearful, I blurted out, "I'm here to see Mr. Vincent Briggs," with all the authority I could muster.

"And your name is . . ?" he asked, peering at me over round glasses.

Here I hesitated, but eventually mumbled, "Carl Matuski." As he picked up a telephone to call upstairs, the elevator opened and a half-dozen people jammed in. In such a situation, would Adam wait? No, he'd be lightfooted and swift. Taking my chance, I darted among the crowd. The door closed just as the man behind the desk stood up to call me back. With Adam on his way somewhere, there wasn't a second to lose.

At the newsroom two floors up, I stepped into a different world from the day before. Now the place hummed with activity. Phones rang, men talked, typewriters clacked. It was so noisy I couldn't hear myself think. Scanning the room, I spotted him at last, just where he'd been the day before. Vincent Briggs sat at his desk, bent forward, typing with both index fingers flying over the keyboard. No one paid attention to me as I made my way to his corner and desk.

I'd wait until he was finished typing and then introduce myself. That was the thing to do. At least, I hoped so. But when he paused, he didn't look at me, or even give any indication he knew I was there. He muttered something to himself and bent even further toward the paper.

Should I speak? I shifted my weight from one leg to the next. I looked down and twisted my mouth to one side. I waited for him to ask what I wanted, but he said nothing.

Finally, I found my nerve. Clearing my throat, I said, "Mister Briggs, I'm Carl—"

"Shut up, kid. I'm on deadline!" He didn't shift position when he talked but kept his gaze on his typewriter and the story he was writing.

I stood there for ten more minutes, silently wondering if he would ever look my way, worrying that the man downstairs would come up at any moment and snatch me out of Vincent Briggs's "office." I kept thinking of Adam headed to the train station. If Briggs would listen to me, if he could help, maybe there was still time to catch up to Adam and tell him there was no need to leave Portland.

After typing, muttering to himself, peering at what he'd written, and typing some more, Briggs pulled the paper from the machine's roller, stacked it with one other already-typed sheet, and called for somebody to deliver it to "typesetting." Then he twirled his chair to face me and stuck his cigar in the corner of his mouth. "All right," he growled, "what do you want?"

As he waited for me to speak, he unrolled his shirt sleeves, revealing stiff cuffs through which heavy gold links had been threaded. All the well-constructed explanations flew out of my head as I faced this "ace reporter"—this giant of the newspaper world. With him glowering at me, I was a stammering imbecile. I was sure whatever I had to say would sound stupid and hardly worth a moment's notice.

Somehow, I found the words, though not the ones I'd originally planned on using, not the ones about what a "pillar of society" Adam was or how he was "the best brother a boy could have." Instead, I managed to squeak out the barest details of the case. But as I told the story, I noticed Vincent Briggs leaning further forward until, by the end of my tale, he was practically doubled over, his eyes looking up at me, his hands between his knees.

"So this rich family is trying to frame your brother, eh?" he said at last, and I could have jumped up and hollered for joy. Here, at last, was someone who saw, as I did, that Adam wasn't guilty. "Tell me everything you know."

I gave him the information Adam had provided me, about the brothers and the family. And I threw in my own guesses about the maid and butler, even though I didn't know if the Petersons employed such servants. Briggs soaked it all up, nodding a few times as I added details.

"Where you go to school, kid?" he asked.

"I . . . I don't," I answered, unsure why he'd ask such a question. Then I noticed one of the Sister Lucretia broadsides on the corner of his desk. Briggs had written a single word on it— "Klan?"

"But I work at the Academy—St. Mary's," I said.

"You like it there?"

"Seems like a good school." Then, to make sure he understood I wasn't still a student, I added, "It's a girls' school. Anyway, I'm done with all that. Needed to help the family."

"What about your brother?"

"Uh . . . he works, too. Odd jobs."

"Where's your brother now?" he asked.

"I . . . I don't know." I wasn't about to tell him Adam had skipped town.

"Well, if I'm going to do this story justice, I really need to talk to him." He leaned back, placed the cigar on the edge of his desk, and scrunched up his mouth to one side. "No good without interviewing the suspect." He started to shift his chair toward the desk again, which I took to be an act of dismissal.

"Wait!" I cried out. "I'll get him to talk to you. If I do that, will you help?"

Briggs looked at me as if I'd uttered a profanity. "I don't help anybody, boy, except the truth. If your brother's innocent, then that's the truth I'll serve. Have him get in touch with me." With that, he turned completely away, and began pawing through the piles of papers on the side of his typewriter as if I'd never interrupted him.

As I left the newspaper office and walked home, I murmured silent prayers of thanks—every prayer of gratitude the nuns at home had taught me and then some. *Thank God! Thank all the saints in Heaven and Mary, too.* Briggs *would* write the story!

All I had to do was find Adam so Briggs could talk to him.

Maybe he hadn't left yet. Maybe he was still at the train station and I could catch him and get him to talk to Briggs before leaving. But as I headed up the broad avenue toward the station, I was stopped in my tracks by Officer Miller.

"Shouldn't you be at work?" he asked. "Or is it one of your Holy Days? Which one is it today, kid—the Feast of Saint Caviar?"

At the mention of the phony saint from the *Cedar School* book, my breath caught. It was one thing to read those hateful words, but another thing entirely to hear them spoken. He'd probably said St. Casimir or St. Caspian, right? I looked at Officer Miller, trying to find the truth in his doughy face. Officer Miller didn't like Adam, but it wasn't because of that stupid book, was it? How many people had read it anyway? How many people would go to hear this Sister Lucretia talk? A day ago, I thought no one could possibly believe this crap. Now I wasn't so sure.

"Uh . . . I'm just running an errand for my uncle," I murmured, looking down.

"Well, if you should happen to see your brother on your way, give him a message for me," Officer Miller said. "Tell him he's not going to see any money from that jewelry, so he might as well turn himself in now and get it over with."

I stared at him. "What do you mean?"

"We're going to be telling every jeweler and pawn shop in town that the Peterson jewelry is missing and what it looks like. As soon as your brother tries to sell it, we'll track him down," Officer Miller said.

"He won't be selling it," I retorted, "because he didn't steal it." I turned to leave, but as soon as I walked away, I realized my trip to the train station had to be postponed. With Officer Miller watching where I was going—I felt his gaze burn into my back—I couldn't lead him to my brother.

Find another way, my inner voice shouted. I couldn't continue toward the train station, but if I looked uncertain, Miller would know I was up to something. I kept walking, not sure where I was heading. *Find another way. Another plan. Adam would keep walking like he knew where he was going . . .*

I rambled through city streets, unsure where I wanted to head. I wanted to talk to Adam, to Vincent Briggs, or anyone who could help me. Most of all, I wanted to be away from Miller. Looking over my shoulder, I didn't see him tagging after me. I cut down a side street and up and around into town. I walked until I was on Sixth, where I hid myself in a crowd.

Eventually, Union Station loomed before me. I hadn't seen it since we'd arrived in Portland. Its striking tower and sprawling red brick buildings set off a torrent of unease. I wished I could get on a train, and if I found Adam, maybe that was the thing to do—just get on a train with him and start our plan a little early.

Taking a deep breath, I walked ahead, making my way into the busy station. How had Adam known which train to take? I looked around for someone to help me, but no one gave me a second glance. They all knew what to do and where to go. I didn't. I felt like a sailor lost at sea, forced to navigate entirely on my own. For a moment, I felt the same sense of hopeless discomfort I'd felt when we'd ridden the trains to Portland in the first place.

I forced these feelings back. If Adam could find his way, so could I. Matching my pace with that of the people around me, I headed toward a large ticket counter. When my turn came, I asked the clerk in a strong voice, "When's the next train leave?"

A short, balding man, he laughed before answering. "Which one? Southern Pacific, Union Pacific, the Cascade line, or the Red Electric?"

"Uh . . ."

"Where you want to go?" he asked.

"I don't know," I said, my confidence faltering. "No, I do know. Baltimore."

After consulting a schedule, he told me I could get a train to San Francisco that afternoon and switch to other trains from there.

"Any other trains to San Francisco?" I asked.

"One's just about ready to leave," he said. "Track 8."

"Thanks!" I shouted, turning back into the station.

"Hey, kid," he called after me, "you need a ticket to get on!"

But I wasn't getting on. I was just trying to find Adam. Gazing at the numbers above the doors lining the room, I found the one for Track 8 and ran for it.

The huge train, hissing and rumbling, sat on its tracks. A few stragglers made their way through open doors, uniformed conductors helping them step on board.

I scanned the full length of the train. A figure near the end caught my eye. There he was! A bundle in one hand, tan cap on his head—Adam! I still had time.

Running forward, I called out, "Adam, wait! Adam! Don't go!"

The train hummed and hooted. Noise filled the air. He hadn't heard. He placed his right foot onto the train, handing his ticket to a conductor. My legs pumping, I sped toward him, screaming at the top of my lungs.

"Adam! Wait! Adam!"

As he made the final step onto the train, he sensed or heard me, and turned toward me, his face twisting into a mask of confusion.

I halted. It wasn't Adam. It was some other fellow.

"You need help, boy?" a red cap asked me.

Startled, I shook my head. "No, no thanks," I said. Catching my breath, I watched as the long, heavy train puffed and screeched away from the station. I peered at the windows, hoping to see Adam's face. If he was on board that train, I couldn't find him.

Feeling totally defeated, I shoved my hands into my pockets, my shoulders slumping and my mouth shaping itself into a grimace. I walked away from the tracks, back toward the station, trying to think of a new plan. By the time I reached the street, my energy and confidence were fading fast. I was beginning to feel it wasn't possible, that everything was stacked against me.

All right, if I couldn't get Adam to talk to Briggs, maybe I could do the next best thing—gather enough information from others associated with the crime to help the reporter with his story. And when Adam finally contacted me, I'd be able to tell him the coast was clear.

I slipped down a side street and headed home, first stopping at Jasluzek's. We didn't have a telephone at Pete's house, but Jasluzek had one. He had let me use it to call Pete's boss one morning when Pete was sick. I entered the store and stood before the counter as Mr. Jasluzek wrapped up a piece of chicken for a stout woman with a dark scarf tied under her chin. When she left, I looked out the door to see if Miller was still behind me. Sure that I was alone, I pointed to the telephone at the end of the counter.

"Please, Mr. Jasluzek, may I use your telephone? It's an emergency." I wasn't lying. My brother's fate hung in the balance.

With skeptical eyes, Jasluzek stared at me. Before he could answer, another woman entered the store, heading for the meat counter.

"Just be quick about it, boy," he said, turning to the customer.

Standing by the counter, holding the cylindrical receiver in one hand and the phone base in the other, I got the operator to connect me with the Peterson household. Keeping my voice down so Jasluzek couldn't hear, I asked to speak to Rose when a stiff-sounding woman answered the phone.

"Whom may I say is calling?" the woman asked archly.

"Carl—" I stopped before giving her my last name. After reading that stuff in the *Cedar School* book and hearing how Miller talked about us being "Bolsheviks," I didn't want her to know I was Polish. "A friend," I said at last. "Just tell her it's a friend."

In a second, a sweeter female voice came on the line. "Hello?" she said, sounding kind of shaky.

"This is Carl Matuski, Adam's brother. Listen, I don't have a lot of time. I need to talk to you soon."

Soft as a whisper, her voice slightly trembling, she responded after a pause, "How is he? Is Adam all right?"

"As fine as he can be, with the cops after him."

I heard her take in her breath like a gasp. "Does he . . . does he ask about me?"

Come to think of it, Adam hardly ever mentioned Rose, but I imagined that was because of the burglary charge her family wanted to hang around his neck. Not wanting to hurt her feelings, though, I muttered a quick, "Sure," then pressed my case. "Look, can you meet me somewhere?"

After a moment's hesitation, she answered. "All right. I can meet you at Meier and Frank's Tea Room. Do you know where that is? At noon. Tell Adam I want to help him."

Chapter Seven

Meier and Frank's was one of the city's best-known department stores. Located at Fifth and Morrison, it was a bustling place of commerce, with awnings over wide display windows facing the street, and at least ten floors filled with all sorts of goods—everything from gleaming perfume bottles and shiny toys to neatly-folded clothes. Its treasure-box of items just made me hurt for wanting them. I'd only been in the store once, right before Christmas the year before.

When we'd first come to Portland, Pete had taken us there to pick out a holiday gift. I had the impression Pete had remembered almost too late that we might expect gifts on Christmas Day. It was a strange outing, filled with disappointment. I was still afraid of Pete, who hardly smiled, and picking out a gift for myself was not the treat I'd thought it might be. The store was crammed with last-minute shoppers, and as I looked around at what to buy, a sad realization hit me. There'd be no other gifts, no little wrapped packages under a decorated tree, like there'd been when Ma was alive. During that visit to the store, I kept thinking how different it would have been with Ma. Nothing Pete did could have made up for that.

When I picked out a stiff new baseball mitt, Pete stared at the price tag and asked if I was sure there wasn't something else

I'd like. Adam whispered in my ear that maybe I should look for something more practical. I ended up picking out a plain cotton shirt with a soft collar, which made Pete smile.

Now I raced past shelves of shirts, racks of women's clothing, and displays of fine china and silver, and headed for the elevator that would speed me to the Tea Room. Today the crowds and atmosphere didn't bother me. I had a goal.

My self-confidence got rattled as I stared into the big restaurant on the tenth floor. Hushed and busy, it looked like a palace from a faraway land—tables with crisp white linens, serving trays pushed by silent servers, and potted plants filling out the room. Serving women in black dresses and filmy white aprons glided up to tables carrying silver trays. Men and women—mostly women—sat and smiled, sipping tea and eating things I wouldn't even know the name of.

A stately woman in black with a large purple pin and bunching lace at her neck approached me. Looking me up and down, she asked, "May I help you?" but didn't seem like she wanted to help me at all.

"I'm—I'm looking for someone," I stammered. When she glanced at my cap, I belatedly remembered to take it off. Swiping it from my head, I looked beyond her, hoping Rose Peterson would see and rescue me.

My wish was fulfilled. Just beyond a large fern at the entranceway, a young woman stood and smiled at me. She mouthed my name and I nodded. With a shy wave, she beckoned.

"There she is!" I cried out, walking right past the startled hostess toward Rose.

I didn't know what to do or say once I got to her table. She was beautiful. No wonder Adam had fallen for her. Her very presence made me aware of all my faults—how gangly and thin I was, how clumsy and awkward I could be. Adam had this way of making you want to be liked by him. On more than one occasion, I'd seen him charm a lady into a shy blush. It didn't surprise me he'd won over someone as pretty as Rose, or that she was smitten enough to meet with Adam's brother on the barest introduction.

Rose's hair was short and wavy blonde, and she wore a suit the color of silvery clouds, with a blouse whose lacy collar spread around her neck and shoulders like a wispy bib. Her face was porcelain pink and her eyes crystal blue, and the way the collar framed her face made me think of pictures of angels on holiday cards, all rosy-cheeked and fresh.

She made me think of Esther, too, back home in Baltimore. Not for the first time since I'd written my letter, I wondered if she'd respond.

"Carl?" Rose said. Her voice was mellow, like velvet music.

I swallowed hard. "You must be Rose," I said, twisting the edge of my cap in my fingers.

With a lace-gloved hand, she gestured toward the chair opposite hers. I sat down.

"I ordered some tea. Would you like some cake?" she asked, scanning the room for the server.

"That would be fine." When I scooted my chair into the table, my knees bumped hers and I immediately apologized. Her face and mine reddened and she looked down at the table.

"How's your brother?" she asked softly.

I didn't want to give out too much information about Adam, so I just said, "Fine, I guess."

Still not looking at me, she asked the same question she'd posed on the phone. "Has he spoken of me?"

No, but he should have, for goodness' sake. She was as pretty as a movie actress—prettier than most girls, in fact. If she'd been sweet on me, I'd have talked about her to anyone who would listen.

"Yes," I stammered, not knowing what else to say. "He says you're real nice." That was true to a point. While Adam had never said those precise words, his voice had betrayed his affection. My heart went out to her—here we both were, trying to fix Adam's problems, when he might well be making more trouble for himself.

Satisfied with my answer, she smiled.

"I can't stay long," she said, pulling off her gloves, revealing pale fingers with rosy pink nails. They made me want to hide my own hands, with their grubby fingernails and calluses.

"My mother will be meeting me in a half hour," she said.

I took that as my cue to begin, so I launched right into my explanation. "I need some information about the night the jewelry was stolen."

Immediately, she shook her head slowly back and forth. "We don't know exactly what night it was stolen." With watery eyes, she looked at me. "That's part of the problem. Mother keeps those things in a special case, which she doesn't check every day. When she went to transfer them into a new safe, she discovered they were missing." She gave me a determined stare. "I don't believe Adam took them. If he'd needed money, he could have just . . ."

She didn't need to finish. He could have just asked her for cash. She was so trusting, so eager to help. I wondered if she'd given him money on other occasions.

"When was the last time your mother saw the jewels?"

"The police asked the same thing," Rose said. "And Mother told them she'd worn them to a dinner party three weeks ago."

Three weeks ago! Adam had only known Rose for two weeks! My foot started to tap with excitement. "Do you have any servants? Did any tradespeople come to the house?"

She nodded. "We have a maid and a cook, but they've been with us since I was a baby. They've never done anything like this.

Mother would never suspect them of it and neither would I."

"People sometimes fall on hard times," I said, but Rose shook her head fiercely.

"No. If they needed extra money, they'd ask for it. Mother has been very generous with them." Rose shifted in her seat, and I could tell she was nervous about something. She kept frowning and opening her mouth to speak, then closing it again as if thinking better of it. We both remained silent as the server arrived with our tea, setting a teapot in front of us along with a plate of little sandwiches—some that looked like chicken and cucumbers, some rare roast beef, all with the crusts cut off the bread. I was hungry, but too nervous to eat. Besides, it was Friday—no meat is allowed Catholics on Fridays. After the server left, I leaned into the table again.

"Anyone else? Any gardeners, roofers, handymen?"

"No! None of those!" Rose said emphatically. As she sipped her tea, her hand shook. I drank some tea, too, eager to find out what she wasn't saying.

"All right," I began again, "how about your brothers—are they hard up for money?"

She smiled, not taking offense. "Evan's a scamp, but he's never been in any trouble. Besides, he's been away all month visiting our grandparents in Eugene. And Bernard is . . . well, he'd never do anything to hurt Mother."

Not wanting to hurt your mother doesn't always translate into honesty, so I pressed her for more information about Bernard.

"Has he ever been in trouble?" I asked.

She looked down, studying her fingers. "Bernard has moods, but that's all." Her face rose and her eyes met mine. "He served in France, you see—the war. He saw some awful things. He doesn't like to talk about them. And he's never been the same since."

If Bernard had served in the Great War, that meant he was

probably in his early twenties, still young enough to make stupid mistakes. A lot of young people were living it up, drinking and partying, dancing to wild music, or so I'd heard. I didn't begrudge another man a good time, but it made me uneasy to see folks acting like there was no tomorrow. I still believed in tomorrow. And I thought Adam did too.

Rose must have felt the same way about *her* brother. A rush of sympathy warmed me again and I actually reached over and tapped her hand. She smiled at me.

"He sometimes went out with friends," she continued, "and gambled." Her voice became a low hush. "He had to ask Daddy for some money to pay off a debt. Daddy was so angry." Straightening in her chair, she smoothed a stray hair off her cheek. "But that's all done with now. He's married and settled down, and has an excellent job with the Portland Bank. I doubt he even remembered where Mother kept her jewelry."

Nonetheless, I asked about her older brother's whereabouts for the past few weeks. It turned out he had visited the house shortly before the jewelry disappeared, and something about that visit actually brought a tear to Rose's eye.

"What's wrong?" I asked, wishing I had a clean handkerchief on hand, feeling somehow responsible for her tears.

"Bernard and I had an argument the night he was in town—an argument about Adam."

My breath came fast and I sat up straight. "About what in particular?"

"Bernard caught me . . . sneaking out one night to meet Adam." She sniffled. "Bernard knew Mother and Father weren't happy I was seeing your brother."

All the more reason to point the finger at Adam, I thought. Except for Rose, none of the Petersons seemed to like him, and would have been just as happy to have him out of their lives.

"Why didn't they like him?" I asked.

She looked down again. "You know . . . all those things people are saying. My parents didn't like me seeing a . . . a Matuski."

I sat back, the wind knocked out of me. I'd expected her to say he was shabbily dressed or didn't have a good job. Or maybe even that he was too quick to tease. I was ready to defend those faults. But they didn't like him for the same reason folks didn't like St. Mary's Academy and the girls who attended it. Adam was Polish and Catholic.

"Bernard threatened to tell Mother and Father I'd gone out without telling them," she said, wiping her eyes.

"Did he?"

"No," she whimpered, "because a few days later, the jewels were gone and the police were after Adam. He didn't want to upset them even more. He went back home without saying a word to them about it—he just gave me a lecture." She swallowed hard and looked up at the ceiling. "He shook his finger at me and said, 'I told you so,' because he'd warned me that Adam was no good."

Even though I'd never met her brother, I could imagine what that talk must have been like. Adam was no good because he was a "Bolshevist," a "papist," a graduate from the "Academy of St. Gregory's Holy Toe Nail." The things I'd read in that pamphlet that had seemed so silly now made me feel sick.

"Adam's a good fellow," I said, but it sounded weak. "And he's not—" I stopped. He wasn't *what*? A Catholic? Son of Poles? He was both those things. So was I. We shouldn't have to defend ourselves because of them. I shifted in my seat. "You just told me that the jewels could have been taken a week before you even knew my brother." I was angry that her family had been so quick to judge, and accuse, Adam.

"No, no, you don't understand," she said, leaning forward and grasping my hand. "My mother hadn't checked on the jewels for weeks, but they were there all the same. I took them the night I went out with Adam—*I* wore them!"

I spent another fifteen minutes in the Tea Room with Rose Peterson after she disclosed the secret she hadn't confessed to the police or to her mother. Adam had taken her to a speakeasy, and she wanted to impress him. So she'd sneaked into her mother's room that afternoon, removed the jewels from their case, and worn them. Then, when she came back home, she was careful to put them back in the velvet case, exactly where she'd found them the day before.

I found both good and bad in this story. I was disappointed to learn that the jewels did, in fact, disappear at a time when Adam was around, which added to the evidence against him. But other people, perhaps even some seedy types, had also seen the jewels. Revelers at the speakeasy must have admired them. And perhaps Rose, who'd worn them to impress Adam, had bragged about their value as well.

But—Adam? *Speakeasies?* When had he started going to them?

I thanked Rose for her information and for the tea, which I'd hardly touched. Before leaving, she pressed my arm and said, "If you see Adam, please tell him I'm sorry about all this." Her warm touch lingered on my skin.

When I left downtown on foot, I decided that Rose's family might be involved in the theft. After all, if Bernard was so opposed to Rose seeing Adam, maybe he had taken the jewels to sully Adam's reputation, to get him into such deep trouble that Rose would never be able to see him again.

If that were the case, though, why hadn't Bernard revealed to the police that the jewels were still in the household the night before Adam and Rose went out together? Surely revealing that fact to the police would make the case against Adam stronger.

But if Bernard's only goal was to keep Rose and Adam apart, maybe all he needed was this dark cloud of suspicion hanging over Adam. Maybe Bernard would stop short of actually sending him to jail.

Or maybe Bernard didn't take the jewels at all, but knew where he wanted the finger pointed when they went missing. And maybe he hadn't seen Rose with the jewelry on and didn't know it was there the night before it disappeared. I cursed myself for not asking Rose one crucial question: Had she worn the jewelry in front of her brother, or had she put it on after leaving the house that night?

I usually don't think folks are capable of such deviousness, but I was beginning to change my opinion. The lies and distortions in that *Cedar School* book, the talk by "Sister Lucretia" being advertised all over town, the things Officer Miller had said to me, and now Rose's admission that her family took a disliking to Adam because of his last name—I wasn't sure anymore what people would do if they were afraid or angry or bothered enough. Maybe Rose's family was so sure Adam, with his foreign name and different religion, was a corrupting influence that they'd do anything to save her from him, including sending him to jail, or scaring him into leaving town.

I had plenty to think about, not the least of which was the fact that I now had a new piece of information that Vincent Briggs could weave into a terrific newspaper story: The jewelry had been seen by a roomful of lowlifes at some city speakeasy. Surely Briggs would now ask why the Peterson family, and the police, were focusing solely on my brother.

If I gave this information to Briggs and he wrote the story, though, Rose could get into deep trouble with her family for keeping it a secret. And it could also turn around and hurt Adam, because it might mean he was on the scene when the jewels were taken.

Not knowing precisely what to do, I skulked on home, kicking stones and looking at the ground as I went. It was a bright, crisp afternoon with puffy white clouds slowly blowing in from the west, where the river met the Pacific, and the smell of salt water and coal smoke was in the air. Seagulls cawed mournfully overhead, and cars put-putted along busy roads, occasionally honking at horse-drawn wagons. I was so absorbed in my thoughts that I crossed one street without looking, jumping up when a blaring hee-haw from a roadster caught my attention. I scurried to the opposite corner, jamming my hands in my pockets, where I fingered my mother's rosary. As I rubbed it, an unvoiced prayer formed in my mind—*Help me! Help Adam! I don't know how to "look after" him, Ma! He always looked after me!*

When I got home, Pete was nowhere to be found. He sometimes did odd jobs on Friday afternoons, helping a friend who owned a truck to haul trash away or transport furniture and other heavy objects for small fees. Occasionally, he dragooned me and Adam into helping.

Smelling fried fish, I went into the kitchen, where a piece of cod sat in a pan. Pete always made cod on Fridays. Pulling off some with my fingers, I thought about the sandwiches Rose had ordered that afternoon. That was another difference between her family and mine. On Fridays, we didn't eat meat. Rose's religion let her eat whatever she wanted, whenever she wanted.

Not knowing what to do and restless to do something more for my brother, I went upstairs to get some paper and a pencil. I thought I'd write down what I knew and what I needed to find out. It would help me organize my thoughts. I had more information now, and maybe more ways to clear Adam.

When I pushed open the door to my room, my eyes grew wide and my mouth dropped open.

There, sprawled out on the bed, was Adam. He was fast asleep.

Chapter Eight

Worry, anger, and relief battled within me as I shook Adam awake. Yes, I was glad to see him back, and glad he hadn't taken off on our trip without me. But what was he doing home? Why hadn't he used his opportunity to leave town? What had he done with the money I gave him?

"Adam! Adam!" I said as I pushed at his arm.

"Wha . . ." His eyes opened and focused on me. He looked awful. His hair lay in dirty strands against the pillow, and his face was covered with the beginnings of a beard. My nose wrinkled as I took in the odor of his clothes. They smelled like sweat and beer. He'd been gone less than a day, but he looked as if he'd been on the road for weeks.

"Get up," I said, pulling the blanket off him. "And get cleaned up. You're stinking up the room, for crying out loud!"

He wiped his face with his hand and, sitting up, stared right at me. "Thanks for the nice welcome, kid."

"Stop calling me 'kid!' Didn't I tell you that already?" All my anger bubbled up into an explosive speech. "What are you doing here anyway? Didn't I give you the money to hide? What's the matter with you, Adam? Going to speakeasies, taking that nice girl Rose with you? What were you thinking?"

Surprised, he swung his legs around and stood. Running his

hands through his hair, he looked at me with hurt and bewilderment in his eyes.

"Slow down. Why are you talking about Rose? How'd you find out about—"

"I met her—that's how."

"You *what?*"

Ignoring his question, I went on, "I found out there could have been any number of people who saw those jewels and known where they were. She wore them to that speakeasy you took her to."

"Geez, Carl, you playing private detective?"

Brushing past him, I picked up his jacket, which was lying on the floor next to the bed. Our father's pocket watch fell out, and I placed it on the bed so it wouldn't get scratched. Patting down the pockets, I found a few spare coins and nothing else.

"Where's the money I gave you? Didn't you buy a train ticket? Did you miss the train?"

"Yeah. Well, no . . . I mean . . . Carl, at the train station, I got in line to buy a ticket to San Francisco. Then I started thinking I didn't know anybody there—not a single living soul. And even though you gave me a nice bundle of cash, it wasn't enough—not enough to get back to . . . Well, I was afraid, Carl. I didn't know what to do . . ." He looked at the floor, heaving a long sigh. Where was the strong and confident Adam I used to know, the one who'd looked out for me? All of a sudden, it felt unfair to have to look after him, especially when he was doing such a poor job of looking after himself.

"So what happened?" I asked in a slower voice.

"So I sat down in that station and thought. I thought how I wanted to go back to Baltimore—how that's what you and me had planned from the beginning."

At least he was thinking of our old plans. Maybe this was a

sign he was turning a corner, coming back to who he used to be. It was a start. Relieved, I sighed, too.

He scratched his neck and grimaced. "So I tried to get some more money," he said quietly. "I found a poker game on North Avenue that's always on. And I started winning big, Carl, real big. I thought, 'Geez, I can pay for both our tickets *and* repay Carl what he lent me,' so I kept at it."

He didn't need to tell me the rest. I immediately knew what had happened. He'd lost it all—not only all he'd won when his luck was running good, but all the money I'd given him in the first place. He'd lost it because he was trying to get enough for *both* of us to leave together. The old Adam had been looking out for me, but not the right way. It had twisted into something perverse.

Standing in our narrow room at that moment, I felt like a ton of bricks had fallen on my back. I felt pressed down, and I didn't know how to move without upsetting something. It occurred to me that sometime in the past year, my brother, once a happy-go-lucky fellow with the smarts and know-how to help me out and protect me, had gotten lost, turning into someone who needed me to protect him. It must have happened gradually and I'd been too absorbed in my own dreaming to notice. I wanted to tell him he'd made a mistake figuring he could count on me—that I stumbled along from day to day with no thought of how to turn plans into reality, that I looked down at my feet making sure one was in front of the other, while Adam scanned the horizon and told me where to go. It was hard mapping out a future. I wanted him to be the older brother he'd always been, the one who charted the course. We'd made a good team that way.

Why had he changed? Had he started to believe all the bad things people said about "our kind"? Did he really think he was no good just because he had a funny last name and went to a different church? When did people start believing those things, and why hadn't I noticed that either?

Here again was something Adam used to do for me. He'd read the newspapers, and he listened to men talk. He'd told me what was happening in the world. Me, I preferred losing myself in adventure stories, books about cowboys and war heroes I borrowed from the school when I could. That's why I didn't pay attention. Adam had always done it for me.

I couldn't think about all this too long, though. His predicament left no time for long talks about what to do and why everything had happened. Who knew when Pete would come home, or if the cops would come around again, asking if I'd seen Adam? For all I knew, Adam might not have been careful heading home. Miller might have caught a glimpse of him.

"Get cleaned up," I said grimly. "There's somebody I want you to meet."

If nothing else, I could take Adam to talk to Vincent Briggs, so the reporter could write that big story about Adam being framed.

And maybe one other thing: I'd start paying attention now to what was in those papers I delivered every day.

—————◦•✧•◦—————

It took some effort to track Briggs down on a Friday night.

The newspaper was practically closed by the time we got there, and I had to find Briggs's home address and convince Adam it was worth the time to talk to him. Adam resisted mightily, sure nobody would believe his side of the story—it was best for him, he said, to just get away as soon as he could get some more money. He looked scared, tired, and sick, and he wasn't thinking straight.

In the nearly empty newsroom, I found a late-working copy boy, a short, thin fellow who wore wireless spectacles. He looked busy and gave me a glance that signaled he didn't think we were worth much attention.

I turned to Adam. "Tell him we have a hot tip for Vincent Briggs and need his address."

Adam looked at me as if I'd asked him to jump into the river.

"You're older," I explained. "He'll give it to you."

"This isn't going to help," Adam said, turning to leave. "Let's go."

"No, wait!" I took a deep breath and strode with false confidence across the newsroom toward the copy boy myself. He looked up again when he saw me approaching, but his face didn't move. I told him I needed Briggs's address, and spouted out something about a story Briggs was writing and how this information couldn't wait.

The boy paused and squinted at me, but didn't hesitate long before pulling out a paper and pencil.

"You were here the other day," he said. "I remember you." He wrote the address down and handed it to me. I hadn't expected it to be so easy and smiled broadly when I showed the address to Adam, as if this feat would prove we were on the right track.

Still, Adam was reluctant. Briggs's home, it turned out, was near the Irvington district, which was where the Peterson brother lived. Adam wanted nothing to do with Irvington, but we had no choice. We had to talk to Briggs.

It was a long silent journey through a brilliant dusk—the sky was turning a bright shade of rose, as if there'd been a silent explosion beyond the horizon. It was a good while before we stood in the midst of stone and brick mansions, with their neatly clipped bushes and glossy shuttered windows, and the light had faded by then.

"This is stupid," Adam said, grimacing at the house as if it insulted him.

Afraid we'd come all this way just to have Adam turn tail and run, I grabbed his arm and pulled him towards the house. "Come on, you'll like him." At least, I hoped Adam would like him. I hoped it would all work out—this plan I was concocting as I went along. Adam's resistance shook the small portion of confidence I was beginning to build up. Soon, we stood in front of a dark green door, where I used a brass knocker to announce our presence.

When the door finally opened, it wasn't Briggs greeting us, but a tall man in black suit and white gloves, who imperiously asked us what we wanted. Before I had a chance to scrape up my courage and answer him, Vincent Briggs appeared in the tiled hallway beyond.

"The Matuski boy," he said, rushing forward. "That's all right, Devlin," he said to the man who'd answered the door. As Devlin disappeared into the back of the house, a gaily dressed woman walked out of a nearby room.

With a feathery shawl and shiny bandeau around her short wavy hair, she looked like an actress ready to take to the stage. When she saw me and Adam at the door, she laughed and said to Briggs, "Isn't panhandling illegal in this area, darling?"

"Go back to the party, Pauline. Newspaper business," Briggs said.

"Why do you insist on keeping that job, Vince? You don't need the money!" Someone from the other room called Pauline's name, and she retreated. Briggs rolled his eyes and scowled, stepping back to usher us into a room to the right of the doorway.

It was a quiet, cold study with bookshelves all the way to the ceiling and a big polished desk in the corner. Adam and I sat in cloth-covered chairs while Vincent took his place behind the desk. Dressed in a formal black suit with white waistcoat and bowtie, he looked important—I wondered if he and his crowd were preparing to head out for the night. As soon as he sat down, he reached for a wooden box on his desk and pulled out a long, fat cigar. Closing his eyes, he drew it under his nose, and when he opened his eyes again, his face had settled into a look of contentment.

"Coffee?" he said, searching a drawer for a match.

"No, thank you, sir," I said. "This is my brother, Adam. I said I'd get him to talk to you and—"

Puffing on his cigar, Briggs waved two things away—the smoke and my words.

"Yes, I surmised as much. Let's get to the point, shall we?" He leaned into the desk and found some paper and a pen. I told him all I'd learned, and Briggs wrote, sometimes asking questions directly of Adam.

"Why did you see the Peterson girl on the sly?" he asked. His tone was so sharp and pointed that I thought I'd been duped and Briggs would turn on us as well.

Adam squirmed and answered in just as sharp a tone, "Well, that's obvious, isn't it?" He fingered the frayed collar of his jacket, as if to say, "We're poor. The Petersons aren't."

"The Petersons wouldn't want their daughter seeing a Matuski," I added, proud of myself for my new awareness of politics.

As the questioning continued in that uncomfortable vein, I began to realize what Vincent was doing. He was making sure he understood the story. He was trying to get to the "truth" of it.

To my disappointment, Adam didn't say much during the questioning. He spent most of the visit staring at his hands and twisting his cap through his fingers. His answers were short, and he never volunteered anything beyond what Briggs asked. But Briggs wrote it all down and assured us he'd make some calls and run the story on Monday. Before we left, he shook our hands, and I felt important.

"Do you need a ride home?" he asked at the door. "I could have Devlin take you."

"No, thank you!" Adam piped up. I looked at him, surprised. Adam was forgoing a ride in a car? He must have been awfully nervous. I echoed his thanks, and we were on our way.

Adam stared at the ground while he rushed ahead of me. When I caught up, I asked what was wrong.

"I don't like this, Carl," he said at last. "What I need is less attention, not more of it. And how do you know what he's going to write? You heard the questions he was asking. It could make things worse."

"He's a good man, Adam," I insisted, pulling on his arm. But he shrugged away. "He's an 'ace reporter,'" I said, repeating the phrase I'd heard at the newspaper.

"So what?" Adam said, hunched over with his hands dug into his pockets. "He's one of them."

I knew what he meant. By "them," he meant people with money, people like the Petersons, not people like us. Adam had already been wronged by their kind. No wonder he didn't trust them. Had I made a mistake here? Was I a fool to trust people like that? Once again, I found myself wishing I didn't have to take the lead, and that Adam would step back into that role for the both of us.

Saturday and Sunday were rough. I begged Adam to find a new hideout, but he was tired and sick, with a fever that washed his brow with sweat. Staying at Pete's was risky because, unless Adam was quiet as a mouse, Pete could easily find him. Neither of us wanted to take a chance with what Pete would do. He might bring the cops into it, figuring all would be well if Adam gave himself up. Or he might think Adam deserved some punishment for the speakeasy visits and the drinking.

Adam was so worn out that he slept most of Saturday. I kept the door to our room closed and didn't leave the house all day. Pete slept in most of it, too, and visited the Petrovich widow in the afternoon. When he asked why I was sticking close to home, I followed Adam, feigning illness.

Not feeling well was also my excuse for not going to Mass on Sunday. Pete went without me, which just added to the pile of wrongs I was committing. Usually the two of us went to early Low Mass while Adam ambled off to the ten o'clock High Mass alone. I used to kid Adam about that, about him needing to "get holy," by going to the longer service, after carousing on Saturday nights.

Now those jokes seemed sour. I should have been keeping more of an eye on him. Back in Baltimore, we'd go to Mass together—me, Adam, and Ma. We'd go to the mid-morning Low Mass and sit together in the third pew on the right. While Ma prayed her Rosary, I'd look around for my friends. Sometimes Esther and her family came to that Mass, too.

On this Sunday, I nearly made myself sick with concern, sneaking food up to Adam, watching the street for signs of Miller, and worrying about Briggs's story. Maybe Adam had been right, and Briggs would betray us. I wasn't used to being in charge, and no doubt I was making all kinds of mistakes I wasn't even aware of.

To make matters worse, Pete came home from church angry.

"Carl Casimir Matuski, come down here this instant!" he shouted, bursting through the front door.

Signaling to Adam to be quiet, I closed the bedroom door behind me and scurried down the stairs to Pete.

He was standing at the foot of the steps, his hands on his hips. He still had on his Sunday best—a clean pair of brown trousers and a rumpled herring-bone coat. The fingers of his right hand held a dark gray fedora.

"You like your job—at the Academy?" Pete asked me, his moustache quivering. His face was white and his eyes blazed with irritation.

"Yeah . . . I guess . . ." I answered, not sure where this was heading.

"You know it's a good school run by good sisters?"

I nodded.

"Do you know why it's important to have such a school?"

I nodded again. Catholic schools taught the Catholic religion. Was that what Pete meant?

His jaw muscles rippled. His voice was hard and cold when he spoke again.

"The little ones up the street—the Petrovich girls—they went to the city school," he continued. "The teachers there tried to make all the kids, including the twins, say the same prayers and sing the same hymns—ones the girls don't sing at church."

The Petrovich twins were about five years younger than me.

He raised his hand in defiance, shaking his finger at me. "The Petrovich girls—they would not say the school prayers. They said the prayers your mother said—the prayers I said this morning at Holy Mass!" His voice trembled and filled the room. "And you know what the teacher did? He beat them—hit them on their hands, and made them bleed! In front of the whole class!"

The Petrovich girls were sweet little things. How could anyone think they were bad enough to punish like that, especially when all they'd done was pray a certain way? What had happened to the world when I wasn't paying attention? It was one thing to try and pass a stupid law. It was quite another to smack little girls for their religious beliefs. My fists balled and my muscles stiffened.

Abruptly, Pete stopped, his face contorted, his eyes rolling upward. "I told Mrs. Petrovich I would go talk to the teacher, but she will not let me," he said in a tight voice. I knew he would have done more than talk. "I should go anyway!" He hit the banister with his fist.

I felt like I was seeing something I wasn't meant to see, and it bothered me. My uncle was confessing to weakness. He regretted not giving that teacher a dose of his own medicine. It had to make Pete feel like a coward, not setting the man straight because a woman had insisted. I could understand that feeling—wondering whether you had given in because you thought it was right or because you were afraid. I wanted to pummel that teacher myself. I wanted to beat up all these bullies trying to make folks like us something we weren't. Yet here I stood, as powerless as Pete.

He calmed down and looked at me.

"I help out now. I give money to send the girls to St. Mary's." He grabbed my chin and forced me to look at him. "Why did you tell your boss there you had no time to take down those papers about the woman who claims to be an 'escaped nun'? Huh? What's so important you can't spend an hour helping put out the lies those people say about us? That—that woman—will speak this week to hundreds of people. Hundreds! And you could have helped keep people from hearing her. Just a simple favor your boss asked of you. A simple favor you could not do."

So that was why he was so angry at me. Pete must have talked to Lester after Mass. Lester was no tattler, so my guess was the story came out innocently enough. Maybe, when Pete and Lester started planning how to stop the school vote, Pete volunteered me to help out. Lester would have probably mentioned how I couldn't spare the time, because I'd turned down the chance to remove posters when I was there the other day.

My face hurt where Pete's fingers pinched into the skin.

"Nobody can believe that stuff," I said to Pete in my defense, just as I'd told Lester. But I knew better. People did believe it. And my voice sounded like I didn't mean it.

My uncle snorted in disgust.

I was confused, alone, and afraid, and didn't want to be. "I had to help Adam," I finally said, tired of lying. "I really was busy. I'll help out later. I'll do whatever you want me to do."

Pete looked at me a long time and sighed. He muttered a curse—"*Psiakrew*"—and closed his eyes for a moment.

"I know you love your brother," he said at last, "but you do what Lester asks or I'll take the switch to you. If you don't help out, there might not be a job left for you at that school because there won't be a school at all . . ."

I didn't care that much about losing my job at St. Mary's. After all, I hoped to be working back in Baltimore in short order. No, St. Mary's' fate didn't bother me as much as what the school's troubles meant to my more pressing problem. If people were riled up enough against Catholics to close their schools and hurt little girls, then what hope did Adam have in my fight to prove his innocence?

Chapter Nine

All that day and night, I thought of the story my uncle had told about the little Petrovich girls and the city school. They were little angels with hair the color of autumn leaves whose corkscrew curls bounced when they ran. They were always full of fun and smiles, and not for one second could I see them as troublemakers or disobedient pupils in need of a harsh lesson.

I saw them sitting in a classroom, practically swallowed up by their desks, taunted by a bully of a teacher with a knuckle-rapping ruler in his hand. I wondered if the teacher had made fun of their name, and talked about "St. Caviar." I wondered how I would have felt if my teacher had shamed me that way, especially in front of my brother. And I felt as Pete must have felt—my hands clenching into fists, eager to take on that teacher and teach him a lesson or two.

Pete didn't say much to me the rest of the day. On Sundays, he tried to cook something special, but all he made for supper that day was potato pie. I couldn't look at him. Every time I did, I saw his disappointment. I started to think I was turning into something bad by not living up to his expectations for me, and I wanted that to stop. Maybe that's how it happens—you turn bad little by little, by not doing things you're supposed to do or doing things you're not supposed to do. And then when you notice, it's too late.

———— ❖ ————

On Monday, I woke up with a nervous ball in the pit of my stomach. I felt like I'd eaten something rotten and had to keep swallowing to stop myself from spitting up. As I waited to read the evening paper, I didn't know how I'd manage to get through the day.

But I had more immediate things to worry about. I had to go work at the Academy or Pete would be angry, and I had to make sure Adam was safe for the day.

The house was quiet when I woke up. Pete was already at work. The overcast sky was filled with clouds pressing down so far I felt like I could touch them if I stood on tiptoe. The air smelled damp, like rain coming. After getting dressed and drinking a little milk—I couldn't stomach much of anything else—I nudged Adam awake.

"I'm going to work," I whispered. "You stay here and out of sight. I'll stop home before my paper route. Don't let Pete see you." He grunted in agreement and I left.

When I showed up at the Academy, I came across a timid-looking woman standing at the entrance. She seemed to be Pete's age, and was neat and prim in a brown dress with matching sweater and hat. She held a piece of paper and a bag out in front of her, and the way she twisted up her mouth made me think she needed help. I was in a hurry, but something about her reminded me of Rose—a slightly forlorn expression and the shimmer of fear in her eyes—so I asked if she needed anything.

When I spoke, she jumped, so lost in thought that I startled her.

"Is this how you get to the office of St. Mary's?" she asked, pointing straight ahead to the front stairway, which led to porticoed doors. I usually went in a side door to meet Lester, but I tipped my hat to her and offered to show her the way.

"Thank you," she said, following my lead. As we scurried up the steps, she became friendlier. "This is my first day teaching. Are you a student?"

At first, I was a little offended that she thought I was young enough to be one of St. Mary's students. Besides, it was a school for girls. But I brushed it aside—she was nervous, after all, and probably just trying to make conversation.

"No, ma'am," I said, holding open the heavy door so she could go through. "I work at the Academy."

I pointed her on her way and headed downstairs to Lester to see what work he had for me. I found him sitting on a stool, reading some papers and smoking a cigarette. When I came in, he looked up and smiled.

The smile put me so at ease, an apology slipped right from my mouth—a genuine one, remorse without shame.

"I'm sorry I didn't help out," I said, twisting my cap in my hands. "With the posters, that is. Do you have any other work like that? I'll do it on my own time."

He stood and placed his hands on his hips and looked around. "I'm going to be re-plastering a wall in the third floor classroom," he said, sweeping his hand behind him, still clutching the papers. "On the back of the building." He looked down at the papers and scrunched up his mouth, thinking.

"Here's what you can do," he said slowly, tapping the top of the three pages. "Take this to the printer—as you go into town, there's one two blocks over and up. Have him run off a hundred copies or so. And then—" He stopped and thought. "Then leave them around town, in stores and such. Anyplace people gather."

He handed me the sheets.

Confused, I looked them over. It was a "pastoral letter" from the archbishop, about why the proposed School Law was a bad thing. It was the type of thing we usually heard about only in church.

I looked at Lester. "Do I tell the printer to send the bill to St. Mary's?"

He grimaced, shook his head, and pulled some bills from his pocket. "See if they'll do it for this." He handed me a wad of money.

My eyes widened and I stepped back. Lester's own money—it didn't seem right to take it, didn't seem right he had to pay to counter lies about us. As if reading my mind, he said, "That's money a group of us collected for something like this." He scratched his chin. "I don't think any of us could put things better than Archbishop Christie."

"I can give some money, too," I said, wanting to help. I had some coins on me, and I wouldn't have to tell Adam or Pete what I spent them on.

"That's good of you, Carl, but you keep your money."

"Maybe the school can give some," I said eagerly. "They just hired a new teacher. They must be doing all right." I told him how I'd run into a woman on the way in, but instead of cheering Lester, this news had the opposite effect—he sighed and slowly shook his head.

"That would be Elsa Richter. She used to teach at the public school in your neighborhood. They fired her out when they found out her own children didn't go there."

My jaw dropped open. "Who fired her?"

"The Ku Klux Klan. They made things bad for her—bad for the people who hired her." He didn't say any more and turned to pick up his wooden toolbox.

But I stood stock still, trying to think of something to convince him he had to be wrong, or exaggerating. I still didn't want to believe that people would be so quick to judge, to do others harm. Yes, I'd come to see how easily some could be fooled by "Sister Lucretia" or *The Old Cedar School*. But here was an example of folks going from foolish thoughts to mean-spirited action.

"The Klan," I said at last, "can't be that powerful."

Lester gave out a laugh, but there was no mirth in it. "Our next governor may well be a Klansman," he said. "He's running real strong right now."

He came over and patted me on the shoulder. "You do that chore for me and call it a day, son."

"But the plastering .. ?"

"It's a one-man job. I'll tell the sisters you're running errands for the school."

I placed my cap back on and left. As I found my way to the printer, I took the time to more carefully read the letter in my hands. Archbishop Christie made the case for why the Catholic schools were just as good as the public ones—why they were just as "American." He used six points to prove it, but they didn't make me feel any better—only worse.

Catholic schools were "absolutely American," he wrote, because "their history" was American, "their curriculum" was American, "their teachers" were American, and "their pupils" were American. He even emphasized this point by saying in big capital letters that ENGLISH was the language spoken in these schools, even though they taught kids with different nationalities. "The ideals" of these schools were American, and even their mottos ("For God and country") were American.

I stepped up my pace and puckered my lips into a grim frown. The archbishop shouldn't have to write that stuff. My free hand balled into a fist. Why didn't people know these things already?

It was a humiliation to have to write it all out! The archbishop was lowering himself to say these things, practically pleading with folks to accept Catholic schools as being just as good as public ones. He shouldn't have to do that, and a big part of me wished he hadn't—it humiliated me.

I would do as Lester asked me, but I wasn't at all happy or proud to pitch in this way.

———⋅◦✦◦⋅———

Doing the job took me into late afternoon. While I waited for the printer to finish, I walked around town pulling "Sister Lucretia" advertisements from poles and walls. Lester and his friends had done a good job getting most of them, but I found a good half-dozen in my search. Then I spent some time waiting for the ink to dry on the letters the printer had run through his noisy machine.

Time crawled by as slow as tugboats in the harbor, and I wasn't in the mood to rush it. As I left the letters on counters and tables at stores and restaurants, I carried my anger with me. I borrowed a few tacks from the printer and even put some of the letters up where I'd found the "Sister Lucretia" posters earlier, taking a righteous satisfaction in clobbering the tacks with a rock as I pounded out my rage.

When I'd handed out the last of the papers, I felt wrung out, as if I'd worked a long day of hard labor. My muscles ached, and my jaw was stiff from clenching my teeth. It rained softly that afternoon, and the wet, cool air helped revive me. Now I was free to fight my own battles in my own way, and that meant finding the evening newspaper. It had to be out by now, and the closest place to see it was a store across the street from the Academy.

I ran faster than I'd ever run before. I was so desperate to see the *Telegram* that I plunked down my own hard-earned coins for a copy, even though I'd be picking up a stack of newspapers to deliver in a few minutes.

Heart racing, I scanned the front page. Nothing. My hopes sank. Walking home to check in on Adam, I flipped through page after page, searching for Briggs's story. Had he given up, thought better of it, decided it was no story at all?

"Hey, watch it!" a tall man with an umbrella cried out as I ran into him.

"Sorry," I said. Frowning, I stopped and looked through the rest of the paper.

And there, at last, I saw it. On the front page of the city section, in big, fat black letters: "CATHOLIC BOY FALSELY ACCUSED?" I breathed out a welcome sigh of relief. Here, at last, was an argument I was comfortable with. It wasn't the pleading defensiveness of the archbishop, but an attack on those who were attacking us! Thank God for Vincent G. Briggs! Thank God for the *Telegram*!

With each word I read, my spirits rose. Briggs had not only written the tale, he'd done it in such a way there could be no doubt Adam was innocent.

Briggs must have called the Peterson family, because Mr. Peterson was quoted in the story saying he "distrusted that scallywag Matuski from the moment I saw him." And Briggs discovered that Bernard Peterson, Rose's brother, did indeed have some financial debts to pay off.

But what was even more interesting was how Briggs connected the story to the bigger one—the one that Lester and Pete and the archbishop were concerned about.

"That boy is precisely why we're having to vote on the School Question," Mr. Peterson was quoted as saying. "He's a vagabond and probably a Communist to boot, picking up who-knows-what kind of ideas in that Catholic school he and other poor unfortunates go to."

In the article, Briggs explained how the School Question's supporters wanted all of Oregon's children forced into one kind of school—public—so they could learn to be "true Americans." If the measure was approved by voters, St. Mary's and all other religious schools—even plain old private ones—would be shut down. It would be illegal to attend.

By the end of the story, you were convinced not only that Adam was innocent, but that he was being singled out because he was a poor Catholic—persecuted by the very same folks who supported the School Question.

With a broad smile, I sprinted towards home to show the story to Adam.

As I rounded the corner toward home, a voice shouted, "Whoa, boy, what you running from—a fire?" I had to stop in my tracks. Officer Miller stood in my way. He pointed to the newspaper under my arm and said, "I don't have to guess who was behind that tall tale, now, do I?"

"Adam's innocent," I said, staring at him as if daring him to fight. Briggs's story made me bold. With the city newspaper backing my claim, I felt like I could take on any bully—even one in a policeman's uniform. "Vincent Briggs is the paper's ace crime reporter," I added for effect.

Miller bent back his head and let out a hearty laugh. "Vincent Briggs writes stories fit for a novel—fiction through and through."

"He does not," I said, wishing I could think of something more clever to say. I wanted to tell Miller his story about "St. Caviar" was fiction. I wanted to tell him he was wrong about me and Adam and all Catholics—that the archbishop shouldn't have to defend us.

A thousand phrases burned on my lips. But my anger jammed them up and kept them locked away. It was just as well. If I let my anger get the better of me, I might say something I shouldn't about Adam.

Instead, I walked right past him, headed for home. He called after me, "Don't think you made any friends with that newspaper story!" He laughed. "That Polack brother of yours is still in big trouble! And I *will* find him!"

With each step, my shoulders grew straighter and my stride stronger. Walking away, ignoring his taunts, felt like one of the best things I'd ever done.

Chapter Ten

Vincent Briggs's story had me flying high above the clouds. It justified everything I'd tried to do for Adam. I'd used my smarts to fix a problem, and now everything would be all right.

Adam would be excited—he'd have to be. I envisioned him patting me on the back and telling me I'd done a great job. I imagined him smiling, even laughing, saying things would be different now, that *he'd* be different, like he used to be.

I imagined my mother smiling down on me.

So I was surprised and disappointed when Adam hardly changed expression as he scanned the small type. He sat on the edge of his bed, joylessly reading the story. He frowned instead of smiled.

"Well?" Still in my coat and hat, I couldn't help asking as he folded the paper closed.

He looked up at me and smiled slightly. "It's a pretty good story, that's for sure," he said softly. Pete was downstairs.

"It'll help, don't you think?"

"How?" he asked, staring at the wall as if something else was on his mind.

"Well, the police will have to look into other folks now. The whole city'll know it."

Adam let out a quick sigh and shook his head. "Maybe. I don't know, kid."

I was about to protest when he stood, looked past the door, and asked, "What's Pete doing?"

Just like that, in an instant, he forgot the story, like it didn't matter for either of us, like all my hard work meant nothing. My lips tightened. I waited for him to acknowledge my success. I kept waiting. Nothing. Instead, he looked restless, like he was getting ready to leave.

I wanted to argue with him, but I couldn't find the words. What would I say? "Tell me I did something good"? I'd sound like a baby. I shouldn't have to ask for praise—he should offer it. *Tell me I did a good thing, Adam,* I thought. *Help me help you. Come back to me!*

"I don't know what Pete's doing. Maybe napping," I snapped. "What do you care?"

"I'm going crazy here," he said. Turning, he pulled a jacket from the end of the bed and patted down the pockets. He was looking for money. "It's like a cage, Carl. I have to get out and get some air."

I ground my teeth. Going out was dangerous. Adam could be caught whenever he stepped outside, and now he was blithely talking about "getting some air." Who would rescue him if he was caught? Me! I'd have to do it. Just like I'd been doing everything else so far.

"You can't!" My voice rose and Adam's eyes widened. "You have to stay here, where it's safe. Let me see what I can find out on my newspaper route today. Maybe I can find you someplace else to stay."

"I know of 'some place,'" he said, hooking the jacket over his shoulder.

I didn't like the sound of that. "You mean some place like the one you took Rose to?"

His lip curled up in a cynical smile, but by not answering, I knew he was going to search out some of his lowlife friends, maybe have some fun at a speakeasy. I was trying to save him, but he kept making things worse.

"Just stay here," I said forcefully. "Don't mess things up while I'm trying to fix them." It was like I was the older brother. "I need to do my route and when I come back, I'll get you some food. While I'm gone, I'll seek out a new hideout. But don't go anywhere, Adam. Not yet."

———

That afternoon, I threw myself into my newspaper route with an energy I hadn't felt since the first day on the job. The activity was good for me. The cool air numbed my anger and cleared my head.

Adam's attitude was a problem, but not the most immediate one. First, I had to think of a place where Adam would be safe. Our room probably *did* feel like a cage to him, and he *did* need some place better to stay—some place he could move around freely. I even thought of going to Vincent Briggs to see if Adam could stay with him, but then I remembered what a posh house Briggs lived in. He might have enjoyed writing up Adam's story, but Briggs would probably turn him in.

My route took me past our church, a big gray stone building with arched oak doors and a spire that pierced the sky. The church! That was it! The chapel in the basement of the church would be closed tomorrow for renovation—I'd heard about it for weeks. If Adam could wait one more day, he could hole up in the chapel at night, protected in a locked sacristy that went untouched by the work crews. It would be warm, from the heated church above, and far more spacious than our cramped little room. Just one more day—that's all he had to wait.

With one problem down, I moved on. Briggs's story had revealed that Rose's brother was in debt. Officer Miller had said the police were on the lookout at pawn shops and jewelry stores where the jewelry might be sold. But Bernard Peterson might not know that. If he'd taken the jewelry to generate some quick cash, he could have sold it already. I wanted to find a way to contact jewelers myself, as a double-check on whatever the police discovered. I no longer trusted anyone except myself to clear Adam.

On top of all that, I still hadn't given up on the idea that one of the Petersons' servants could have committed the crime. Rose might think they were trustworthy, but that didn't necessarily mean they were. How could I find out where they lived?

On the way home, I stopped at a store and bought my brother a chocolate bar. It would be a peace offering. Maybe Adam just needed some cheering up.

Later, at home, Adam and I ate dinner in the kitchen. Pete had gone to some meeting at the church, so I'd roused Adam and told him to come downstairs. Although I'd planned on talking to him about my ideas, his dour mood brought mine back as well. We fed ourselves in silence.

After a while, however, Adam pointed to my plate.

"You're not eating much. You're afraid Pete will figure out I'm here," he said.

He was right. I was only eating a little, nervous that Pete would know I was hiding and taking care of Adam. Shoving my half-empty plate forward, I shook my head. "Naw, I'm just not that hungry, that's all." My stomach growled.

Adam laughed, and just like that, he was my brother again, the fellow who looked on the bright side, who didn't want harm to come to me, but didn't make me feel weak for needing his protection. Back in Baltimore, he'd laughed like that when a bully had chased me home from school one day. By screeching out the boy's name in a high-pitched voice, he'd tricked him into thinking his mother was coming after him. I laughed at Adam's imitation and my own narrow escape.

Adam pushed my plate back toward me and threw his own drumstick on it.

"Huh?" I said.

"I'll get something to eat later," he said, licking his fingers.

I stared at him before greedily devouring the chicken. He was right—I *was* hungry, and the food sure tasted good. "Where?" I said, between bites. "Where you going?"

"Just out." He stood and took his plate to the sink. "I told you I'd go crazy if I stayed here."

"I understand that, Adam, but . . ." And then I told him about the chapel. "Just one more night, Adam—that's all you have to stay here." I didn't like the way my voice sounded—kind of high and whiny, like I was afraid he'd say no and disappoint me.

With his back toward me, he said, "All right. It's just one night anyway." Whistling a happy tune, he washed our dirty dishes. When I was done eating, he did mine, too, and his cheerful generosity made me suspicious. As I watched him, I realized, sadly, that I didn't trust him.

———◦•◦••◦•◦———

I didn't want to believe Adam would put himself in danger, let alone lie to me. But as I lay on my bed that evening, I was convinced he was going to sneak out of the house. My throat and chest tightened and my eyes burned. My muscles ached from staying still. I wanted to walk away from the house and let the cool air freeze my fears away.

I puzzled through the past year, trying to figure out when Adam's fun-loving spirit had turned into something risky. I couldn't identify the moment, though, when he'd turned that corner, when he'd stopped being helpful, strong, and happy.

Things happen so fast in life you don't realize something important is going by. Or maybe it's that things happen too slowly and we don't take notice because we expect the big moments to be accompanied by fireworks. Instead, they glide past us so peacefully that we're tricked into thinking everything's as easy as the passage of time itself.

Adam's change had occurred as smoothly as that, when I wasn't paying attention.

Maybe I should have helped out more during that time, instead of just waiting for him to lead. Why hadn't I pulled my weight before? Maybe it had all been too much for him to bear alone. If I had tried harder then, maybe he wouldn't be in trouble now.

If, if, if . . . maybe, maybe, maybe. The possibilities swirled in the night, making me drowsy. But I had to stay alert.

It was hard pretending I was asleep without actually falling asleep. I managed to do it by blinking my eyes real fast and keeping the blankets off so I'd be cold. About an hour after I'd turned out the light, I heard Adam moving off the bed. He sat silently for a few moments before getting up, probably to make sure I was really asleep. I kept my eyes closed. I breathed steadily.

After he'd moved stealthily into the hallway and down the stairs, I jumped out of bed and grabbed my own clothes. Hopping into my pants, I nearly stumbled down the stairs, but I had to be quick or I wouldn't see which direction he'd headed. A sock in one hand and another between my teeth, I peered out the back door. Outside the house, he'd made a right. Quickly, I wriggled into my shirt and put on my scuffed shoes. Grabbing my jacket from the hooks by the back door, I was off, following him into the darkness.

Damp air pricked at my face and neck as I quietly tracked him. I was careful to walk on grass or dirt whenever possible so he wouldn't hear my footsteps behind him. Once, when he stopped and listened, I hid behind a tin trash bin. He headed down Fourth and over Morrison toward Broadway, then hopped over a rickety fence that surrounded an old house in the middle of a block of similar dwellings. It was a bad section of the city where police often patrolled. Adam was risking arrest by coming here—and for what? What was so important to him?

Music drifted into the night from somewhere deep inside the house, and light framed each window, escaping dark shades.

Hiding behind the fence, I peered through a slit, observing him. He walked up to the door and knocked, using our "secret" knock—the one he'd suggested I use when he'd found the empty building to hide in. A few seconds later, the door opened and the music grew louder. A small jazz band was playing "Ain't We Got Fun." As the tune drifted into the night, though, it sounded sad and empty, like someone trying to keep away bad spirits by pretending to be carefree. A burly figure looked up and down the street, then let Adam in.

I stood, breathing hard and swallowing my fears. I had to get in there. But what if I was mistaken, as at the train station, and the figure who'd entered wasn't Adam? It was dark and hard to see. I could be going into a bad place—a place where they shanghaied fellows to work as sailors on ships. What if that heavy figure at the door gave me a good beating for trying to enter? What if they asked me questions I couldn't answer, or made fun of me, or called the police?

But I had to do it. This could be the speakeasy where Adam's friends had seen him with Rose the night she'd worn the jewels. I'd done a lot so far, I reminded myself. I'd talked with Vincent Briggs, I'd found his home, I'd helped Lester. This was one more thing on my list. I could do it. I had to. Hadn't I just been worrying about how I hadn't helped Adam enough when he needed me? This was my chance. I shouldn't expect it to be easy.

Squaring my shoulders, I walked up to the door. Next to the doorbell was a small sign: Café Parisienne. Smoothing my hair, I pulled myself up to try and feel as adult as possible. Then I raised my hand and knocked, using that special pattern, the one Adam had made sure I remembered.

Seconds seemed like hours. Maybe they hadn't heard. Maybe I'd used the wrong combination. I had just raised my hand to knock again when the door flung open. This time, it wasn't a man standing there but a woman, and unlike any I'd ever seen. Her unnatural whitish-blonde hair framed a face heavy with makeup. Her natural eyebrows were gone, and new, thinly arched ones drawn in their place. Her lips were ruby red, and she wore a white satin dress that came to the hems of her rolled-up stockings, revealing dimpled knees. When she saw me, she giggled, clutching a cigarette holder in her right hand.

"You must have the wrong address. This isn't a school play yard!" Her speech was slurred and I detected the same whiskey-like odor that had been on Adam's breath the other day.

She started to close the door, but I boldly stuck my foot in the way. I wasn't going back—not without finding Adam and getting some more information. "I'm older than I look," I said, trying to deepen my voice. "And I'm here with Adam." I nodded inside.

After shrugging her shoulders, she opened the door wide to let me pass. Inside, a small foyer opened onto a restaurant, where a few patrons sipped from tea cups, talking and laughing. Why had Adam come here? Was he hungry?

The woman brushed past me and I followed her down a narrow hallway next to the front dining room. After pushing open a door, she leaned forward and said something to a heavy-set man, which I couldn't hear over the music. The man nodded and the woman led me in.

"There he is," she said, pointing to the far side of another room.

Unlike the front room, this one was dark, smoky, and noisy. Small round tables were crammed against one another, and a pianist and other musicians played jazz on a little stage at the far end. Adjusting to the lack of light, I focused on Adam, hunched over one of the tables, talking intently to a red-headed girl dressed much like the one who'd answered the door. A bottle and two glasses sat before them.

With all the noise and movement, Adam didn't notice me until I was standing right in front of him, and then he jumped out of his chair.

"Holy Christmas!" Adam said, standing. "What are you doing here? How'd you even know—"

"I followed you," I said.

"Well, you shouldn't be here, Carl. Go home!" Adam looked uneasy, but I wasn't going anywhere. I wanted to haul Adam out of that place and give him a licking. But I needed to be stronger than my own worst feelings, and I needed to find out more about the theft.

"I'm not going home. I want to meet your friends," I said, nodding to the woman at the table. I wanted to meet all of them—and find out if they might have seen Adam bring Rose to this joint, or seen her jewels before they were stolen.

Reluctantly, Adam gestured to the woman. "This is Lillian," he said. And to her, he said, "This is my brother, Carl."

"Nice to meet you," she said, smiling broadly. "Adam never told me he had a brother."

I slid into a seat opposite her and Adam. "How long you been coming here?" I asked Lillian. I figured she'd tell me more than Adam would, and besides, I didn't want to talk to Adam just then. I was too angry.

He frowned at me as I talked to Lillian.

"Oh, I found this place a year ago," Lillian said. "And then your brother and me, we just kind of met recently and liked each other . . ." She looked shyly at her hands.

If Adam was sweet on Lillian, what about Rose? I looked at Adam, who was no longer looking at me.

"You have a lot of friends who come here?" I asked Lillian.

"What? You mean me and Adam? Why, sure." She smiled proudly. "We have a whole gang. Right, honey?" She looked at Adam, who grimaced.

"Like who? Maybe I know some of 'em, too," I said.

Adam lifted up his face. "You won't know them," he said.

"I might," I pressed.

Lillian was only too happy to oblige. She rattled off a list of names. "Anton, and Mark, and Paul, and there's Jonesy . . . but he don't come around much anymore."

"Why not?"

She tilted her head and her smile fell. "Some trouble or something."

"What trouble?" I asked.

"Well, they say he was taking money from a bank where he works . . ." She tapped her fingers on the table.

I perked up. Adam was hanging with a crowd of bad types—

and one of them might already be in trouble with the law. If this Jonesy fellow had been at the speakeasy the night Adam brought Rose in wearing the jewels, he could have decided to make some easy cash by burglarizing her house.

"Tell me about this Jonesy," I said to Lillian.

Adam was about to silence her, but she prattled on. "Oh, he's a gentleman. Real fine clothes and from a good family. He didn't need no job in a stupid bank, if you ask me, so I doubt he's feeling the pinch."

"Was Jonesy here the night you came in with Rose?" I asked, looking at Adam now.

Adam glowered at me. "I dunno," he said.

"Who's Rose?" asked Lillian, looking at my brother.

"A girl Adam knows," I said.

"A friend of Carl's," Adam lied.

Leaning back, Lillian stared at my brother, confused. Faith won out over doubt, and her smile returned, lighting up her cupid-like face. "Yeah?" she said, turning to me. "Well, you should bring her by sometime. We could have a good time together! Does she like dancing?"

"No," I said at the same time Adam said, "Yes." Lillian looked from Adam to me and back again. Then she sat back and said nothing.

"C'mon, Adam, try to remember," I said. "Was Jonesy here that night?"

"He was here most nights," he said reluctantly. "So yeah, he was probably here that night."

Lillian pursed her lips together as her brows wrinkled. To me, she said, "How come *your* friend Rose came here with Adam instead of you?"

Adam and I exchanged glances. Obviously, he didn't want Lillian to know about Rose. When it became clear I wouldn't lie for him, he turned to Lillian and said, "Rose is *my* friend. Carl's trying to help clear my name of that Peterson jewel theft. Rose was wearing the jewels."

Lillian's face turned almost as red as her hair. Crossing her arms over her shimmery dress, she stared at Adam through narrowed eyes. She'd figured it out.

"I'm sorry," he said without looking at her. With a huff, she stood and walked away.

"Now see what you've done," Adam said to me. "She was a good girl."

"I thought you liked Rose!" I said, exasperated.

"I did like Rose. But her parents weren't going to let us see each other," he said sadly. Looking over his shoulder at Lillian's retreating figure, he let out a sigh.

"Where's this Jonesy guy anyway?" I asked. There was no time for sympathy, even if I'd been in the mood to give it. "If he's in trouble with the law, maybe he thought about taking Rose's jewels."

Adam shook his head slowly. "Carl, stop trying to be the police. You can't—"

"Just tell me his name—Jonesy *what?*"

Adam sighed again. "Reginald Jones. Everybody calls him Jonesy. He worked at Portland Bank. He's probably long gone by now."

"You don't know that for sure," I said. Portland Bank—hadn't Rose Peterson said her brother worked there? Was that just a coincidence?

"Nobody's seen him for a few days," said Adam.

"Since the robbery?"

He shrugged. "Maybe."

The band struck up a fast number and I saw a dashing fellow in crisp gray trousers and slicked-back hair ask Lillian to dance.

Adam followed my gaze, looking morosely at the girl I'd made him lose.

"C'mon," he said after a few seconds watching the couple dance. "Let's get out of here."

⸻•⸻

We walked home in silence. Adam jammed his hands in his pockets and kept his head down. I kicked at stones along the way, wondering when I'd get a chance to track down this Reginald Jones fellow, and if Adam would care. A hundred speeches passed through my mind. I wanted to ask him what had happened to our plan to go back East together and how he could muck it up without feeling bad. I wanted to ask him why he no longer felt the need to look out for himself, and why I had to do it for him. I wanted to tell him how disappointed Ma would be in him.

But I said nothing. If I was to get my brother back, it would be through deeds, not words. Clearing his name, I decided, would turn things around and make him take a fresh look at his life, make him think good things were possible again. It would get him back to that crossroads where he could choose better things for himself.

As we neared our street, I found something new to worry about—sneaking Adam back into the house without waking up Pete.

Sneaking around, lying, tracking down clues—it all came back to Adam. I looked over at him. His face was glum, his shoulders hunched. Pity washed over me. If only he hadn't gone to speakeasies, run with bad crowds, and met Rose. But how could meeting a sweet gal like Rose lead to trouble? How could he have known? Because of something inside him, he must have been ready to take chances instead of playing it safe. Because of something inside him, he had decided to stop trying to be good.

When we turned the corner for home, I picked up the strong smell of smoke in the air. Looking up, I saw a glow in the distance. At first, I thought there might be a fire. If so, there would be fire-fighters and policemen around—not a good crowd for Adam to wander into.

"Hold on," I said to Adam, putting my arm out in front of him. Adam, however, wanted to see what was happening. Picking up his pace, he moved ahead of me until he stopped just a block from our house. Next to an old oak tree with a thick trunk that obscured the walkway, he stood transfixed.

Ghosts, white-robed and swaying, stood chanting in front of Pete's house. Their voices created an ominous hum, a murmuring hiss like a swarm of bees ready to attack. They bunched together, a white blur of luminous spirits.

But they weren't spirits. They were something worse—men who didn't want to be seen or known, dressed head to toe in white sheets. Pointed hoods hid their faces, and through round holes cut in their masks and hoods, their eyes appeared as glowing coals. They stood in two rows in front of Pete's house, which was lit by flames leaping up a burning cross.

One of the men, who had a special emblem on his robe, stepped forward. "Adam Matuski," he called out in a deep, clear voice, "come out and take your punishment like a man."

Fear licked up my spine like the flames on the cross. My hands grew clammy. I couldn't swallow. My eyes widening, I pulled my brother behind the tree and out of eyesight. Stupefied by the sight, he didn't resist.

"Who are they?" I whispered to Adam.

"The Klan," he whispered back. "They're members of the Ku Klux Klan. They must've read that article in the paper about me.

Oh, jeez, Carl."

His voice was high and shaky. I'd never heard him sound so afraid, and that rocked me to my core, but I couldn't blame him. There was something dreadful about a group of men hidden behind costumes—they could do anything, and nobody could hold them to account because you wouldn't be able to say who did it. That had to be the reason for their robes—so they could do horrible things and nobody would ever put a name to a face.

To my horror, the front door of the house opened and Pete stepped out. I wanted to shout for him to go back in where it was safe, but instead I just watched as he walked to the edge of the step and stared back at the crowd. His hair stuck out like pieces of rough hay, and his shirt was unbuttoned, but he tightly gripped a coal shovel in his right hand.

"Get out of here or I'll call the police!" he yelled, waving the shovel. Several of the Klansmen laughed, and I found myself lunging forward to help Uncle Pete. But Adam pulled me back.

"Are you crazy?" he hissed at me.

"But Pete . . ."

"If Pete can't handle them, we're not going to be able to do much either."

Another robed man stepped toward the burning cross. Pointing his right hand at the house, he yelled, "Go ahead and call the police. That's what we want—the police to arrest your thieving nephew!" A rumble of support came from the crowd.

Pete stood silent for a moment, and in that moment, I was deathly afraid for him. What if they tore him to pieces before our very eyes? What if I was too scared to help?

God, how I wanted that cross to stop burning! I wanted to run up, find a bucket of water, and extinguish the flames. The cross seemed like a brand, searing into the night sky our "sin" for all the neighbors to see—that we were Catholics, with a foreign-sounding last name. I wanted the clouds to open and a flooding rain to pummel the earth, dousing the flames. Wasn't that what happened in the Bible stories we'd heard about in school? Why couldn't it happen now?

Without a word, Pete pulled himself up. For a second, he closed his eyes and breathed deeply, before opening them again. His lips pressed together in a thin line, and he strode down the steps toward the cross with such forcefulness that a few Klansmen actually moved back.

He swung the shovel hard toward the burning posts of the cross, knocking them to the earth, then quickly shoveled sod and dirt until the cross fire was out. I wanted to cheer. A few Klansmen came near, and he swung the shovel at them, forcing them back. Sweating, he leaned on the shovel and wiped his brow.

"Get out of here—all of you!" he yelled in a ferocious voice. He waved the shovel wildly toward the crowd, and his voice was part growl, part speech. He shouted something in Polish I'd never heard before, something that sounded like a curse. "Robert and John and yes, you, Jeffrey. I know who you are, you cowards. Adam's not here. And even if he was, I'd make you get him over *my dead body*."

When he lunged again toward the crowd, those in the first row fell back.

"Go on!" Pete said.

A hush descended over the mob, forced back by Pete's ferocity. Finally, the lead Klansman spoke.

"We'll be back, Pete. Mark my words. We'll be back. You make sure that boy gives himself up. He's a disgrace to the city!"

The crowd trooped off into the night, away from us and away from the house. No longer menacing, their retreating figures looked silly, like children in costumes. I could breathe again.

"I can't go back," Adam whispered to me.

"I can sneak you in," I said. "Besides, you heard Pete—he won't give you up!" For all that had happened, this realization was a happy and unexpected one. Pete had bucked the Ku Klux Klan to protect Adam. I'd been wrong about Pete. He wasn't as warm or welcoming as our mother had been. But he cared about us.

"Naw," Adam said, glancing up the street, where the last of the Klansmen walked away. "That was cause Pete was cornered. He thinks I should give myself up to the police."

Whirling around to face Adam, I grabbed his arm. "Pete's talked to you about this?"

Adam looked down at the ground. "Yeah, just after it happened."

"And what did he say?"

"He said no good comes when you run from the law."

I didn't know what to say or do. I'd just witnessed a terrible exhibition of raw power, of men taking the law into their own hands. How could Pete be sure that Adam would receive fair treatment if the authorities took him in? Officer Miller was no friend of ours. Why assume other officers would be fair?

"C'mon," I said at last, "let's at least talk to him."

Adam pulled away and backed off. "No. You go on home. I'll get a message to you . . . tomorrow. I'll find a place to stay. Don't worry about me!"

Then he disappeared into the night, his swift footsteps echoing in the distance.

Chapter Eleven

I continued to worry about Adam. He was my brother, and I'd added to his troubles. Just as he'd warned, the attention from the newspaper article had brought danger, not aid.

I snuck back home that night, creeping in the back door. I took off my shoes and tiptoed up to my room, closing the door behind me slowly enough to keep the hinge from creaking and the latch from clicking. I kept the light off as I undressed and fell onto my bed.

I knew I must have slept, because time passed and I didn't remember how it did. When I awoke, I heard Pete stirring downstairs. But I could tell from the light under my door that it was past dawn. Hurrying as if I had a deadline to meet, I went to the bathroom and washed up, then dressed and went downstairs to the kitchen.

It was a gray day and the kitchen was bathed in a milky light. From somewhere far away, I heard the full-throated toot of a ship's horn. Much closer, old Thomas's horse-bells jingled as he made his way through the Portland streets, his last rounds of the season.

Pete stood at the stove, frying some eggs. "You hungry?" he asked without turning.

"I guess," I said, slipping into a seat at the table.

For a few more seconds, he cooked in silence. Then he turned toward me, with two fried eggs perched on the end of a spatula. I took that as my cue to help and scooted up to grab plates and forks. When I set them on the table, he delivered the eggs to my plate, then pulled a piece of toast from the oven and placed it beside the eggs.

After I dove into *my* meal, he cooked his own and sat down across from me. He looked tired, even haggard. Dark circles colored the underside of his eyes, and his skin had a pasty, unhealthy hue to it. His eyes were red and watery, and his hair was as disheveled as it had been when he'd confronted the Klan. Even his moustache twisted this way and that, hairs sticking out like pieces of straw.

I wanted to tell him how proud I was when he stood up to the Klansmen. But I couldn't. I couldn't let him know I'd seen it.

"You not going in today?" I asked softly.

He looked up. "Going in late," he said.

"I . . . I thought I had a dream last night," I said. "I mean, I thought I heard something . . ."

Pete gave me a quick sour smile. "Just some hooligans making trouble. I set 'em straight."

I nodded. "Yeah, I bet you did, Uncle Pete." And I smiled.

He smiled back.

Before work that day, I scanned the day's newspaper. There was no mention of the Klan gathering on our street—no tale of the outrageous burning cross.

There were stories about the School Question, though. In

one, the "exalted Cyclops" of the Portland Klan argued that children who didn't go to public schools had to be taught a "uniform outlook on all national and patriotic questions." Bolsheviks had already "infiltrated" the education of Ukrainian citizens in Toronto, Canada, and that sort of nonsense had to be stopped at the border. Everybody knows, this "Cyclops" said, that Catholics are just waiting for the Pope to tell them what to do to take over here in America.

It was a bunch of manure, and I was furious that the "Cyclops" didn't give his name to the reporter. I wasn't sure who I was madder at—the Klansman who hid behind the white sheet of nothingness, or the reporter who let him get away with it.

I felt better, though, when I saw another article in which Archbishop Curley of Baltimore—*my* Baltimore!—declared that the Oregon School Law, if passed, would follow the very same Karl Marx principles people like Officer Miller accused people like me of supporting. It amounted to "state socialism," the archbishop said. I wished I could show Miller the story.

After reading the newspaper, I hurried through my route, did a slap-dash job repairing a broken back step for Pete, and told him I was going out to meet a friend. In reality, I was going downtown to find out what I could about Reginald Jones—the "Jonesy" fellow Adam and Lillian knew.

My first stop was the Portland Bank, a big red-brick building with gilt-lettering on the windows and frosted panes on the front doors—the *locked* front doors.

The downtown bank was open only until three-thirty each day, it turned out, and it was nearly an hour and a half past that now. Gazing through the window, I tried to figure out what to do next.

Chances were that nobody at the bank would tell me much about Jonesy. Chances were they'd be embarrassed to talk about a worker who'd gotten into trouble.

But if it had been a lawbreaking offense, the newspaper might have written it up. Why hadn't I paid more attention to the paper before now? I'd delivered it for months!

Taking a deep breath, I rushed off toward the *Telegram* building. On our "tour" of the newsroom, Gus had mentioned something called a "morgue"—a place where they kept old newspaper articles. If something had been written about a crime Jonesy committed, I might find it there.

Hours later, darkness had fallen and I was still in that dusty room, surrounded by old newspapers. After some hesitation, I'd talked my way in, saying I was working on something for Briggs. If anyone checked with him, he might vouch for me. And if he didn't, I might have what I need before getting kicked out. I pored through every paper for the previous month and had started on the month before that when a long shadow obscured my light. Vincent Briggs stood in the doorway, cigar in hand.

"I thought I recognized you," he said. "What are you up to, son?"

After his article, I trusted him, maybe more than I did anyone else. So I told him about Jonesy, and about my other theories. "I thought I'd find something in the morgue," I concluded.

"And you haven't turned anything up?"

"No, sir."

He scratched his head, leaving a tuft of hair standing out at an odd angle above his right ear. Then he absent-mindedly puffed on the cigar, finally crossing his arms and holding his chin with his cigar-laden hand.

"Could be the bank wanted to hush it up," he said, more to himself than to me. "Could be they don't want their customers to know they had a bad apple among the bunch." He looked at me and smiled. "Say, thanks, son, you're becoming a regular tipster," he said, turning and leaving.

I took that to mean he'd look into the story, so I leaned back and closed the paper I was reading, then rubbed my weary eyes. At least with Vincent Briggs looking into the Jonesy story, I could move on to another suspect—the Peterson brother.

Somehow, I had to check out the pawnshops and jewelry stores in the area where Bernard Peterson lived and worked. If Bernard tried to pawn the jewels, I needed to know, just to make sure Officer Miller and his pals didn't ignore the information.

Picking up my cap and shrugging into my jacket, I left for home.

Pete was sitting at the kitchen table when I got home, along with about five other men, all of them smoking and talking. One of them was Lester. When Pete heard the front door open, he looked up and scooted his chair back.

"Where you been?" he said, more out of worry than anger.

"Just out and around," I said, swiping my hat off my head and hanging it on the banister.

"You eat anything?" From the way he asked, I could tell it would be an inconvenience to feed me now. Truth was, I was starving. I'd only had some bread and milk at lunch. I'd been too nervous to eat much. My face must have given me away.

"C'mon then," Pete said, patting me on the back, "there's some sausage and bread."

While I shyly fetched my meal to take to my room, Pete introduced me as his nephew. "He works at the Academy, too," Pete said proudly, looking at Lester, who confirmed that with a nod. The others murmured their approval.

Pete told me they were part of a group the church was putting together—something called the Truth Society of Oregon—and they were going to put out their own pamphlets to counter ones like *The Old Cedar School*.

"Jack here's a Lutheran," Pete told me, "and Orville over there is a Methodist. They're *dobry ludzie*—good people."

I knew what Pete was telling me—that there were fine men out there who weren't Catholic, but who were just as upset as he was about the School Question.

In as polite a voice as I could muster, I said I was pleased to make their acquaintance and asked Pete if I could be excused. He beamed a proud smile at me and nodded. As I turned to leave, he called after me.

"You have a letter," he said. "I put it on the stair."

A letter? I rushed around the corner and retrieved the envelope. Before I even saw the return address, I knew who was writing—Esther!

My plate of food in one hand, the letter in the other, I raced upstairs as fast as I could. I was no longer hungry, at least not for food.

Esther's letter consisted of two pages, both sides overflowing with her neat, sloping handwriting. I read the letter twice before eating and another two times after.

She was "so pleased" to hear from me. She'd been "sad to discover" I'd left town, and no one had known where we'd headed. "Julian's sister thought Adam said something about an uncle in Oregon, though, so I wasn't surprised to see that's where you are now. Where is Adam?"

An odd question to ask—where is Adam? What had Adam told Julian's sister before we left Baltimore?

"I am very happy to learn you will be returning soon," she wrote. "Poppa says any young man willing to work hard can find a job here. If you write and tell me the train you will be on, I might be able to meet you . . ."

And finally, "Poppa and Momma both agreed you could stay in the basement room for a few weeks when you come back. They always liked you. I like you, too."

It filled my heart to bursting. Esther liked me, and had the courage to write it. She'd had the courage to ask her parents to put me up, too. They saw promise in me. They saw a man.

But the letter contained troubling messages, too—ones I couldn't quite figure out. It was clear Esther thought I was alone, that Adam either hadn't traveled with me or was off on some other adventure. Why would she have that idea?

I thought back to what I'd written her. I hadn't mentioned Adam in my letter except to say how well he'd handled our journey west. Most of my letter had been about how much I missed Baltimore and my friends and how I was planning on coming home "real soon." Perhaps that's why she assumed Adam was elsewhere.

I wished I could just pick up a telephone and talk to her. Even if we had a telephone, that would be impossible. It would use up all our money to make such a call.

I looked over at Adam's bed, which offered no evidence he'd returned. His few belongings were gone. The only thing he'd left behind was Dad's old watch. And that looked unintentional—the watch was almost hidden by his pillow. He'd probably gone back to the speakeasy, back to Lillian (while Rose still pined for him), and back to the "gang" who might lead him into who-knew-what kind of trouble.

Or maybe he'd taken my advice and gone to the chapel, where he could safely bunk out for the night.

Imagining him asleep below the church gave me some measure of peace. Although I hadn't considered it before, perhaps staying in the church would have a positive effect on Adam, bring him back "home," to where he used to be—optimistic, eager to take on the world, good.

I lay on my bed, the letter from Esther in my hands. I wanted to write her back immediately. But first, I had to figure out how to handle my next problem—contacting jewelers in the area to see if the jewelry had turned up there. If I could get to them before Officer Miller and the police did, the information would help lead me to the real thief. I didn't trust Miller to do it.

I couldn't cut work, though. Heck, there'd probably be more than the usual amount for me to do, with Lester a part of this Truth Society. My guess was that the Society would have other jobs for me akin to printing and distributing the archbishop's letter. And I couldn't do the jewelry job by phone—no one would lend me a phone long enough to make all the calls.

A page of Esther's letter slipped to the floor. As I bent to pick it up, the idea came to me—I'd write to the jewelers. Writing was the best way to do it, after all. If I wrote to them, I could pretend I was someone else. I could pretend I was a collector or a jeweler myself, someone interested in fine things, and that way, unaware of my true motives, they'd be less likely to lie to cover up any possible wrongdoing.

I folded Esther's letter and placed it in my jacket pocket, then rummaged around upstairs and found some paper. I started to write.

"To Whom It May Concern . . ." I began.

For an hour, I labored. I wrote five drafts of the letter before hitting on one I thought sounded good. I pretended to be a jeweler, writing on behalf of a very wealthy customer "eager to purchase a ruby and diamond set of earrings to wear to a fancy dress ball." I signed my name "Alfred Baguette" because I thought it sounded important—I'd seen the word on a French bakery sign—and I included Pete's address, asking them to write me back if they had anything like the jewels I described.

Now, all I needed to do was get the addresses of jewelry shops and pawnbrokers in the area. There couldn't be that many. Maybe one of the jewelers in town would know.

Yawning, I got up and opened my door. The house was dark and quiet—the Truth Society was gone. Taking my empty plate and glass downstairs to the kitchen, I glanced at the clock above the table. It was nearly midnight! I had to get some sleep, but I had one last task to perform, a job that I looked forward to with sweet anticipation. I went back upstairs and pulled out some more paper. "Dear Esther," I penned, "You have no idea how happy your letter made me . . ."

Chapter Twelve

After posting my letter to Esther the next day, I couldn't help hoping I'd get another from her even before she had a chance to read my awkward note. But the postman didn't have any more letters for me.

If I wasn't looking for the postman, I was alert for Adam's return. Every footfall outside the house had me scurrying to the window to see if Adam was back. And every time, I was disappointed. I had no idea where my brother had run off to. I hoped it was somewhere he wouldn't get into any more trouble. And I hoped he'd come back eventually, after I'd cleared his name, so we could head home together.

My investigation was going so slowly I could scream. Each day, I looked through the newspaper for a story on Reginald Jones and the Portland Bank, hoping Vincent Briggs had come through once again. Tuesday, Wednesday, then Thursday rolled by with no story.

I had plenty to do in that time, though. On Tuesday afternoon, I walked into town and boldly entered the Benson's Fine Jewelry and Gold establishment, acting as if I'd dealt in jewels my entire life. But when the starched and pinched man behind the counter treated me like a vagabond, ignoring my questions about other jewelry stores in town, my confidence was shaken. What did this man know about me and why did he so dislike me? I thought of the burning cross on our lawn. Though I knew in my heart I was guilty of no sin for being a Matuski, I focused immediately on my failings. I was clumsily dressed. I hadn't seen my brother slip away from me. While the jeweler didn't know that last thing, I did, and after seeing that burning cross, any poor treatment made me feel my faults were obvious to all.

I felt this less after my second try, because this time, I fared better. I stopped in the Medlisson pawn shop, and there an elderly man with no hair and a thick accent spent a half hour giving me the names and addresses of a half dozen stores in the area. When he tried to sell me a pin like the one I claimed to be looking for, I feigned interest, still another lie to feel bad about.

Once I had the addresses, I had to copy my letters over and over again and mail them off. This made for an excruciatingly slow letter-writing day at the Academy, sitting on an overturned crate in the boiler room instead of measuring a broken window for a new piece of plate glass.

Lucky for me, Pete was very busy that week, hardly giving me a second glance as I rushed around on my various errands. He was meeting with his Truth Society a couple nights a week now, mostly at the school.

Even with all this activity, I was impatient. No story on Reginald Jones appeared in the *Telegram*. Vincent Briggs had let me down.

All right, then, I thought. Staring out the kitchen window one afternoon, I spread newspapers out before me, searching for the story, but I couldn't focus, thinking instead of missed opportunities. Reginald Jones might be gone soon, and I'd never learn the truth about him. Slamming my hand on the table, I made a decision.

If Briggs wouldn't get the story, I would.

—•◦•◦•—

The next day, I checked in with Lester and was relieved to find he had no work for me. I immediately headed to the Portland Bank before he could find a task or two to fill my day.

Portland Bank was a giant vault sunk into the ground on the corner of Fifth Avenue. Inside, it felt like a mix between a church and a library. Gleaming marble floors, the smell of wood, and hushed voices greeted me as busy men scratched on papers behind gilded grilles. This wasn't my world, and I immediately felt uncomfortable, as if all eyes were on me. I found myself tiptoeing across the floor, trying not to make any unnecessary noise, or any noise at all. Taking off my hat as I approached a teller's window, I felt so out of place that I expected a guard to haul me off any second. I wasn't even sure what to say to the teller, or how I'd say it. I didn't know what I'd do if they wouldn't tell me anything, or if they asked me a question I couldn't answer. I should have had a plan. Once again, I was without a rudder.

The man behind the marble counter, tall and thin with skin the color of a mushroom, stamped some papers and set them aside before glancing at me through the gold-painted grille work. His reddish hair looked hastily combed, and his neck bulged over a high starched collar.

"Yes, may I help you?" he asked in a pinched voice.

Clearing my throat, I responded, "I'm . . . I'm looking for someone. A Mr. Reginald Jones."

He snapped a ledger closed with a whack that reverberated throughout the lobby. "There is no Reginald Jones here now," he said forcefully, looking beyond me for another customer. But I was the only one in line, and he'd just said something very interesting. He'd said, "now." No Reginald Jones was there *now*. It could mean he *had* worked there—something I already knew from Lillian and Adam—or it could mean he was just out today. Why not just say Reginald Jones *used* to work here?

"Look," I said in a sad voice, as helpless as I felt, "I really need to talk to him. I know he worked here. It's about an account he managed for my great aunt . . ."

The man's face relaxed from impassive rigidity to confusion. Tapping his fingers on his ledger, he frowned. "Maybe I can help you," he said. "What was your aunt's name?"

"No," I lied, "only Mr. Jones can help."

The clerk still did not offer up any news about Reginald Jones's whereabouts. "You see, he used to make out her records person-ally . . ." I had no idea what I was saying or even how bank accounts worked. I just wanted to know where Reginald Jones was.

But the man, eyes widened, seemed convinced. "He handled her account personally?" he said. "Let me see . . ." He looked over his shoulder for help, then walked to a nearby teller. For a min-utes or so, they whispered back and forth, until the other pointed toward a desk where a tidy-looking fellow sat.

The man at the desk had hair the color of wheat, and his small eyes looked out from behind rimless spectacles. In his right hand, he turned a new fountain pen over and over, not realizing his fidgeting was causing the pen to leak. Eventually, he grasped his error, spotting the ink on his clean fingers, and his even features contorted into a glare, the right corner of his lip rising in disgust. Carefully pulling a handkerchief from the pocket of his neat gray suit, he wiped his fingers, never looking up at the teller who'd come to talk to him.

The teller nodded my way and the gray-suited man stared at me, his brow furrowed. He asked the teller a question, but the teller just shrugged. The suited man nodded and stood, walking over to a wooden railing that separated the desk area from the lobby. He motioned me over as the teller returned to his station.

"I understand Reginald Jones handled your aunt's account," he said, smiling. Smelling of peppermint and pipe smoke, he extended his hand. "Perhaps I can help you. My name is Bernard Peterson."

Chapter Thirteen

Bernard Peterson—Rose's brother! She'd told me he worked at Portland Bank, but I'd imagined him in some big office upstairs in a velvet chair behind a desk the size of my room. I hadn't counted on running into him now—yet another reason to curse my lack of planning. Though I'd suspected him ever since talking to Rose, I'd had no idea how to investigate him. Now I was staring right at his watery blue eyes. With thin lips, a weak handshake, and a suit that looked as if it was made of the finest silk, he was the embodiment of disinterested wealth. If you'd have asked me to paint a picture of a rich man, his image would have flowed from my brush.

He led me behind the railing to his desk, where he sat, placing his hands together in a steeple before his face. "Now," he said as I sat across from him, "what's your name, and what was your aunt's name?"

It was cool in the bank, but sweat beaded on my brow. I couldn't give him my real name! He'd know I was related to Adam. Thinking fast, I used the most upstanding name I knew, as much as I despised it.

"John Miller, sir," I said in my best good-boy voice. *Officer Miller.*

"And your aunt?"

"My great-aunt, sir," I continued. "Her name is Mrs. Miller."

He smiled and leaned forward. "What's her first name?"

Nothing came to me. I wanted to choose a nice safe name, nothing foreign-sounding, nothing that sounded Catholic or "Bolshevist." *Rose? Lillian?* I couldn't use those names. My mother's first name had been Marie.

"Mary," I said softly. "Mary Miller."

Smiling again, he picked up a pencil and wrote the name on a piece of lined paper. Turning back to me, he leaned casually on the desk, but his foot, clad in an expensive-looking black leather shoe, tapped nervously on the floor. "What sort of dealings did she have with Mr. Jones?"

Looking around the room, I asked, "Where is he? If you don't mind, sir, I'd like to talk to Mr. Jones." I made sure to articulate "Mr. Jones" loud enough for anyone nearby to hear. It seemed to make Bernard uncomfortable.

"Mr. Jones isn't here right now," he said, his voice rising. But I knew he no longer worked here at all. Was Bernard trying to hide that? "You really need to tell me what the problem is." He reached over and grabbed my wrist. Squeezing hard, he stared into my eyes. "What is it Jonesy did for your aunt's account? Was it a loan?"

A loan? When I'd made up the story of a great aunt having an account at Portland Bank, I'd thought only of a regular old savings account—the kind Pete deposited money in once in a while. He had a little book that showed how much he had and how much "interest" he'd earned on his balance. Why did Bernard Peterson think my made-up aunt might have taken out a loan? Maybe Jonesy had worked with loans specifically.

"Uh . . . yeah," I improvised, "I guess . . . I . . ."

He leaned further forward and his voice became a whisper. His nails dug into my wrist and his eyes looked wild and desperate. "Whatever it is, I'll take care of it. I'll fix it. I'm sure it was an unintentional error. Jonesy made a lot of them. That's why he's no longer with Portland Bank."

With his nails in my wrist, his face so close, and his breath so quick, I couldn't think straight. Though we were surrounded by people, he could physically harm me in that cold, impersonal bank, and not a soul would care.

But while his grip on me was tight, his face was drained and his eyes frantic. He was clearly afraid of something—something this Reginald Jones had done.

With a quick yank, I pulled my arm away. "You're hurting me, sir," I said, raising my voice.

Looking around to see if anyone had heard me, he stood, announcing loudly and jovially, so all could hear, that he'd "look into your aunt's account immediately."

When he walked toward a row of cabinets, I wiped the sweat from my forehead. Once he discovered there was no Mary Miller with an account here, what would he do? Had I committed a crime? Could he turn me over to the police?

Glancing back toward the railing, I wondered if I could leap over it and escape before he came after me. But I had to know more about Bernard Peterson, and I needed to find out why mentioning Reginald Jones made him so nervous.

Bernard peered at records beside a row of tall arched windows near the wall. His face puckered into confusion. Maybe he'd already figured out I was fibbing. Maybe not. But it was only a matter of time before he did. *Should I stay or run?* I bit my lip and grabbed my cap. A phone rang at a distant desk and the murmur of customers carried from the front of the bank. In this sea of routine, any move would seem a crime. If I ran, it would have to be quick.

He closed a cabinet and turned toward me, file in hand.

I stood. Now was my chance. I could just leave, mutter, "Sorry, I made a mistake," and escape.

He strode toward the desk, his face a worried grimace.

Go! my mind screamed. Twisting the cap in my hand, I took one backwards step away from the desk.

But I didn't see the teller until it was too late. "Hey!" he cried as I bumped right into him, his stack of papers dropping to the ground, splaying around my feet like oversized confetti.

"Watch yourself!" he said, bending to pick them up.

Bernard was closer now, just one desk away. I had to go. He had to know I was only pretending. I had to move fast, but—

"Could you help me, please?" the teller muttered at my feet. Bending, I scooped up papers at a furious speed. "Watch it!" he said. "You're bending the papers!"

Finally, the papers were in a neat stack. The teller stood and went on his way. Now was my chance to be on mine as well. I could escape into the cool morning sunshine and forget I'd tried such a ridiculous scheme.

Too late! Bernard's black leather shoes appeared before me. As I looked up, Bernard tapped a file in his hand, his jaw clenched.

"Well, we have a problem here," he said.

Chapter Fourteen

A problem? Maybe I could come up with an explanation—maybe say I was mistaken, and my aunt might have had an account at a different bank. But I wanted to talk to Reginald Jones because . . . because why? My mind went blank. *Just get away*, I thought. *Just run—*

"Mary Miller on Pine Street, right?" Bernard asked in a voice smooth as syrup.

Exhaling, I nodded. Thank God I'd chosen a common name for my aunt. I had no idea who Mary Miller on Pine Street was, but she would do.

"And she has a savings account with us, I see," Bernard said, still standing. "We have a record of an old loan her husband paid off before he died. Mr. Jones must have sent her a bill for that by accident. You tell her not to worry. Just tear up any statement she receives about a loan. I've taken care of it."

"Yes, sir," I said, nodding. I could breathe again, and as my racing heart relaxed, I wondered why Bernard had jumped to the conclusion that my aunt had taken out a loan, and that Jonesy had messed it up. I suspected it had something to do with the reason he no longer worked at the bank.

"I'll make sure she doesn't receive any more statements," he said. He held out his hand and shook mine. "Thank you for bringing this to my attention. Portland Bank wants all its customers to be satisfied."

He thought he'd solved a problem, but what was it? He wanted me to leave, but I had to learn more. I suspected the bank had let Reginald Jones go for doing something bad that Bernard knew about. Maybe it had something to do with the Peterson jewel theft. Glancing beyond him towards a pebbled-glass door with "Vice-President" written in arched black lettering, I said, "You've been so helpful. I'd like to thank your boss. Is that him?" I pointed to the door.

Before I'd moved half an inch beyond his desk, Bernard Peterson clamped his hand on my shoulder, his nails again digging into my flesh. "That isn't necessary. He's a busy man. In fact, so am I. Thank you for stopping in and bringing this to our attention. I assure you that your aunt will have no further troubles."

With that, he sat down and pulled some papers out in front of him. But still his foot tapped, and his eyes blinked rapidly.

Thanking him, I placed my cap on my head and walked away. Before I reached the railing, though, I saw him reach for the telephone on the corner of his desk. I pulled a slip of paper, a torn portion of one of the Sister Lucretia flyers, from my coat pocket and dropped it so I could linger. As I bent to pick it up, Bernard whispered into the phone.

"Jonesy, we have to meet," was all I heard before a typewriter's clatter drowned out the rest.

There was only one thing for me to do—follow him. He and Reginald Jones were up to something suspicious. Peterson hadn't wanted me to talk to his boss, even to compliment him. It had something to do with loans from the bank, but how would that relate to the jewel theft? I didn't know. I was getting close, but one important puzzle piece was still missing from the jigsaw. I had to find it.

I'd hoped to make quick work of my visit to the bank, then head to the Academy to see if Lester had found something for me to do. Now I had to hang around the bank all day, waiting for Bernard to leave and meet with Reginald.

It was a boring way to spend a day, and I was tired. More than once, my eyes grew heavy as I leaned against a lamp post just down the street, waiting for Bernard to leave the bank. I wasn't sure if he'd take off work-time to meet Jonesy or wait until the end of the day. I couldn't take a chance. I had to wait.

And wait I did. Except for a few breaks to heed the call of nature, I stayed outside that bank for five straight hours. Sometimes I pretended I was a passer-by, walking slowly past to glimpse through the big glass doors. He was still there. I sat in a nearby cafeteria, sipping at a cup of coffee, ever watchful, jumping up once when I saw a rich-looking man exit the bank. It wasn't him.

I waited until my legs were stiff and my head aching. When the bank closed, I hid in the shadows of another bank's pillared entranceway across the wide avenue. But the tellers and clerks didn't leave for still another hour, their heavy coat collars turned up against the cool air as evening's fingers embraced the city. A few laughed and joked, their bowler-clad heads bobbing as they spoke. But where was Bernard Peterson? Was there a back door he could have used? How could I be so stupid not to have cased the joint and looked for all the exits? It was still more evidence of my weak planning.

But then the front door opened, and there he was, glancing up and down the street, afraid, maybe, that someone might see him.

Shrinking back behind a pillar, I watched him walk to the corner and turn right.

Darting behind a moving car, I crossed the street and ran after him, careful to stay at least a half block behind. If I sensed he was going to look over his shoulder, I vanished into a doorway or behind a parked car. It was nerve-wracking work, but I couldn't afford to lose him—or to be seen.

Late afternoon shadows dimmed the streets. Clouds once again pressed in on the city, making it feel later than it was. The sun would set soon, but still I followed.

Two blocks from the bank, Bernard Peterson stopped. Matching my pace to his, I halted as well, bending behind a big black Buick so he wouldn't see me. Once again he glanced to and fro. Then he climbed into a new Model T. As the engine rumbled to life, all I could do was stare. With him in a car, I could never keep up. Bent over so Bernard wouldn't see me, I ran toward his car as he pulled out into the street.

In Baltimore, Adam had once shown me how to hitch a ride on the back of a delivery truck, standing on the fenders and hanging onto the handles for dear life. We'd only done it one time, though, because it frightened me so much I'd nearly peed my pants. Adam had laughed so hard that I'd had to laugh with him. He said he wanted me to learn to hitch a ride in case I ever needed to get somewhere in a hurry.

Bernard's car wasn't as large as a truck, which posed a problem. How could I hang on without him seeing me? I was, after all, tall and gangly, and the car's gently curving back met the canvas top with virtually no room for a handhold. The wheel-protecting fenders were thin and flimsy. I wasn't sure they'd even hold me.

But as the car picked up speed, I made a quick decision, grabbing onto a latch above the fenders and lifting myself up over the back right wheel. Doubling over below the window, I almost fell off as he veered around a corner and down an open road.

My position was precarious. I couldn't move an inch, or even adjust my grip, for fear of falling off. But if a passer-by, especially a policeman, saw me, he could warn Bernard that some vagabond was stealing a trip. Somehow, I had to shift positions and get inside the car if at all possible.

The nip of fall was in the air and I could hardly feel my fingers, cold from my several-hour vigil. I inched them along the rim of the back of the car between the roof and the chassis, and then lifted myself up to peer through one of the three rectangular back window slits.

Focused on the road ahead, Peterson didn't notice me. But getting into that car unseen would be like trying to sneak a whale onto an open dinghy. Though I was sure I could swing my body around, up, and over the open side, I couldn't imagine a way to do it without Bernard catching me in the act, no matter how swiftly I disappeared into the backseat.

Suddenly, his car picked up speed and careened to the left, down a dark street and over a bridge. Below, I saw the smooth water of the river and the winding railroad tracks beside it. If I lost my grip now, disaster awaited me. Colder air bit my face and hands, and I could barely breathe.

Then my left hand slid down the smooth back, losing its hold!

I hung on with only my right hand—and with the weakest of grips. My fingers pressed along a tiny ledge of metal where the roof met the car's carriage. My body swung outward, and the water loomed far, far below, frigid and deadly.

Pushing my feet back toward the car, I winced as burning pain from my tenuous grip moved up my fingers. With all my might, I swung my body back toward the car, slamming into it with a thud I felt through my elbow and up my arm. But it was enough—I grabbed the back rim again as the car left the bridge and returned to land.

I gave up on the idea of getting into the car and hung on for dear life. I'd just have to hope no observer cared enough to alert Bernard to my presence . . . and that I wouldn't freeze to death before he stopped.

⟡

I didn't know where Bernard was headed, and I lost all track of time. Occasionally, I recognized a landmark, like the Burnside Bridge, as dusk settled in. My hands and feet were so icy they didn't feel like part of me any longer. I was so cold and tired I hardly cared anymore what Bernard had to say to Reginald Jones. Maybe he wasn't meeting him. Maybe he was driving somewhere else—to a friend's house perhaps. Then what would I do? How would I get home?

What a stupid idea this had been. Adam was right. I couldn't play detective. My head ached from the cold and my legs felt like lead.

Miserable, hungry, and frozen, I decided to jump off the next time Bernard slowed or stopped. If he went over another bridge, I'd be finished for sure. I'd have to find Reginald Jones another day. Now, the most I could hope for was a safe and quick route home.

As I waited for an opportunity to leave the car, Bernard turned once again, doubling back, this time heading towards the Willamette River. The car slowed as he entered a narrow street between a field of weedy bushes and a warehouse, finally coming to a stop at the water's edge. Stiff and cold, I was afraid I wouldn't be able to unbend myself and get off the car. But as soon as it jerked to a halt, I fell with a soft thump to the ground. As he pulled up the handbrake, I rolled into a patch of tall weeds near the water.

Blowing quietly on my hands to warm them, I listened for Bernard to exit the car. I heard him rummaging in the backseat for something, and uttered a wordless prayer of thanks that I'd been unable to find a way into the car interior, where he would have discovered me at journey's end, and that he'd stopped before I gave up.

At last, he got out, shoving something into his coat pocket and peering up the street we'd just driven down. He walked a few steps and waited, humming into the shadows, his voice shaky. Pulling a flask from his pocket, he took a quick swig.

Seagulls called to each other and a tug boat let out a foggy whoop. Waves gently slapped against the shoreline and the air smelled of dead fish and brine. We waited together, Bernard and me, but I wasn't quite sure what I was waiting for. Throughout our silent vigil, Bernard took several more sips from his flask, his figure barely visible in the light of a distant street lamp.

In a few minutes, another car crunched along the road and came to a stop. A door slammed shut a few seconds after the motor's hum died away, and a man's voice called out a greeting.

"Bernie, is that you?" Then, closer: "A fine place for a meeting! Did you bring the money?"

Bernard answered him, "Yeah, I've got it, Jonesy. I didn't want to meet anywhere we could be seen."

Reginald Jones . . . was here.

"Well, hand it over, old boy," Jonesy said. "It's blasted cold tonight. And I don't like this neighborhood, if you know what I mean." He coughed. "What the . . . what's that?"

Had I been found out? What had suddenly been noticed?

Raising my head, I looked through the underbrush. Darkness made shadows of each man, but light glinted on something in

Bernard's hand. *A gun!*

"You're too much, Jonesy," Bernard said in a tight, nervous voice. "First, you louse up your job by helping yourself to the cash drawer. Then you blackmail me for having a smarter operation than you. But you made one big mistake, Jonesy."

Bernard's voice was not only frantic but slurred.

Jonesy held his hands up in front of him. "Listen, Bernie," he said, "we can solve this like gentlemen. I know you're upset. I . . . I won't bother you again, all right? Let's consider your debt settled. I'll just go along home now, okay?" Slowly, Jonesy started walking backwards to his car. But Bernard stopped him by raising the gun.

"I knew it would come to this, Jonesy, as soon as you started putting the squeeze on me. You'd have to go. And I've been thinking and thinking about just the right way to do it, but I can't wait any longer. You're greedy. And clumsy. I'll never get out now. You tried to imitate me, didn't you? You set up your own loan scheme, except you opened a loan account for someone who really does have an account at the bank—"

"Bernie, you're talking nonsense! I didn't do anything of the kind!" His voice trembling, Jonesy took another step backward.

"Stop lying, Jonesy. I know what you did. Some fellow came in today because his aunt was getting loan bills—she'd paid off her loan years ago. You stupid, stupid idiot. It wasn't enough that you were blackmailing me. You had to get in on it. How many others are there, Jonesy? How many other loans do I have to fix so nobody comes snooping around?"

"I swear, Bernie, I don't have any idea what you're talking about!" Jonesy's tinny, small voice shook. His shadow trembled in the night air. "I only stole a little cash from my drawer. That's all. And I'm willing to forget the rest. You don't owe me a thing—not one red cent. That was all a mistake. I was stupid. I'll get out of town and forget I ever knew you."

"Tell me the names, Jonesy. Who else did you set up accounts for? I'll have to clean it all up." Bernard waved the gun in the air and Jonesy stepped back again.

"There are no names! I didn't do any loans!" Jonesy sounded like he was going to cry.

"Walk over there!" Bernard pointed the gun toward the river. "I knew it would end this way," he muttered under his breath. "When you first came after me . . ."

"What?"

"Over there! Now!" Bernard shouted.

Jonesy obeyed, walking toward the water, pleading with Bernie to let him go, just as he'd let Bernie's "debt" go. I lost sight of them as they stepped down an embankment. Their voices became muffled, so all I heard was the angry tone, but it had to be more of the same—Bernard speaking of things Reginald Jones couldn't, or wouldn't, admit to. At one point, I heard Bernard yell, "Here's your last payment, you selfish rat," and then a grunt and struggle.

Their voices rose in pitch and strength as they argued in the darkness. I wondered what to do. Should I try to help Reginald? Would Bernard really shoot him? No, he couldn't—he came from a good family and had a good job. Taking the jewels was one thing, but this was different. Yet he'd clearly thought of doing this, only later.

I had to do something. I rose from my hiding place, ready to run for the police.

Then I heard a shuffling sound and shouts of anger until finally a sharp crack split the air, followed by a thud.

My heart took off on a wild gallop, and my thoughts became a blur of fog and sound. The seagulls and the toot of the tugboat blended into a ghostlike symphony ending with the hard clap of the gun. It couldn't be. Bernard Peterson, respectable citizen, wouldn't . . . No, he couldn't have. Not him. How could he?

A pitiful curse floated over the weeds.

A rustling and dragging sound was followed by a muted splash. Despite myself, a gurgle of disgust escaped my lips as I grasped the rosary in my pocket. To keep quiet, I shoved my fist into my mouth.

Dear Lord! Bernard Peterson had just murdered a man!

Chapter Fifteen

More than anything else in the world, I wanted to get away from that spot. Sick to my stomach over what I'd just heard, I wanted to run as fast as my legs would carry me—away from Bernard Peterson, and away from his awful deed.

But I crouched again behind swaying weeds, inching toward the road, stopping suddenly when I heard heavy breathing and swift footsteps come back toward the cars. Holding my breath, I waited for Bernard to drive away. A figure slipped into the Ford and started the engine. But instead of backing out and turning around, the car pitched forward and veered straight for the water!

A few seconds later, another splash echoed off the warehouse walls. What had just happened? After doing Jonesy in, had Bernard just killed himself? I couldn't think about it. I couldn't comprehend it. I had to leave.

Standing erect, I walked to the road, trying to get my bearings. Barely able to walk on my shaking legs, I felt drunk. First, I had to find my way home. And then what? Call the police? Tell Uncle Pete? Get in touch with Bernard's sister, Rose? I had to do something.

Shuffling down the lonely street by the warehouse, I pulled my collar around my neck and shoved my hands in my pockets. As the heat of fear receded, the icy air chilled me to the bone.

I'd almost reached the end of the warehouse block when a noise behind me made me jump. *An engine!* Looking behind me, I saw the two white eyes of a car's headlights speeding my way.

It was as if the car itself had noticed me. It veered toward my side of the street, forcing me back against the wall. There were no weeds here for me to hide in. Pressing my back against the rough brick, I held my breath and closed my eyes, anticipating the heavy weight of the car ramming me. Bernard Peterson hadn't killed himself, and now he was trying to kill me!

But then the car breezed past so close I felt its front fender brush my pant leg. I turned back and ran to the river's edge to see if I could help the soul who'd been shot. But the river held no clues. No body, no car—only the lapping waves against the shore. I ran faster than I ever had—away from the river, away from the scene of a dreadful crime, and most of all, away from danger.

—————•◦❖◦•—————

I wandered for several hours before finally discovering familiar territory. I wanted to kiss the ground of my neighborhood. I was home. I was alive.

But by the time I made my way back to Pete's house, I was also exhausted, defeated, and filled with grief for a man I'd never met. Bernard Peterson had killed Reginald Jones. I'd heard it. I was there. Dear Lord, I deserved punishment now. I deserved all the names an Officer Miller could call me. I'd had enough of lies, too, so I'd have to tell Pete the truth. We could go to the police together.

I pulled myself tall and prepared to take a scolding. As I entered the house, though, I didn't hear a sound or see a light.

It was around nine o'clock—sometimes Pete would be in bed by then. But once he noticed I wasn't home, he'd have stayed up.

I raced for the sink as I entered the kitchen, guzzling down a glass of water. My hands shook.

Turning toward the table, I spied a slip of paper. In pencil, Pete had written, "I went to a meeting. Don't wait up for me. Get yourself a sandwich at Old Mickey's." On top of the note were a few coins.

I sank into a chair. Pete hadn't known I was missing because he himself had been out. Yet, while I stirred up trouble, he'd been kind enough to see to it that I got something to eat.

For the first time all evening, I was safe enough to feel hunger gnawing at my stomach. I found a bread heel and wolfed it down, followed by two glasses of milk. Grabbing a pencil from a nearby drawer, I scrawled a note back to Pete: "Thanks, I ate something here."

Then I went to bed, thinking I'd wait until Pete got home and then confess it all. But it wasn't long before I fell into a deep and tortured sleep, dominated by dreams of the drowning ghost of Reginald Jones, his dripping, weed-enshrouded body emerging from the Willamette River, his eyes popping open and gazing into mine. "Why didn't you save me?" his lonesome voice droned, the sound muffled and deepened by the water in his lungs.

The heavy grayness of yesterday vanished that next morning, replaced by a cool, dark blue sky striped with wisps of clouds. Pete was up and out by the time I arose, so I'd either have to go to the police on my own or wait until I could talk to Pete later. I decided to wait. I could barely think well enough to tie my shoes, let alone reconstruct the events of the night before.

I coughed and sneezed and rubbed my burning eyes all the way to the Academy. I couldn't concentrate on my chores, my mind wandering as I emptied and burned trash, raked up newly fallen leaves, and painted an outside door. I dwelled on the horrors of the previous evening, flashes of memory stopping me in my tracks more than once. Chills and fever washed over my body. My joints ached as if I'd been hit by a bat, and my head throbbed.

By the time Lester told me I could go, I wanted to hobble home and head to bed, losing myself in the blackness of sleep. The thought of Reginald Jones's body in the river made my already churning stomach bubble and foam.

But what if I was wrong about what had happened last night? It was dark. I'd heard voices and noises. I'd seen a car leaving the scene. From that, I'd assumed a murder had taken place.

As I cut the wire on my bundle of papers in front of Jasluzek's store that afternoon, I had to laugh at myself. The late afternoon sun shone and warmed my shoulders. My imagination had gotten the better of me last night—that had to be it. I'd probably heard nothing more than a good fist fight, the cold and my oncoming fever transforming it into a fantastic tale of murder. Why, if I went over to Portland Bank the next day, I'd probably see Bernard Peterson sitting at his desk, calm as could be, as if nothing had happened—because nothing had!

Gus had left a note for me on my papers, berating me for not doing my route the day before. He'd had other boys cover for me, he wrote, and would give them the route permanently if I didn't buck up. As sick as I felt, I had to get the papers out today. I'd rest when I got back to Pete's. I'd clear my head then.

As I heaved my newspapers onto my shoulder, my skin felt prickly and dry, my throat was sore, and my vision blurred. Maybe something did happen after all. If Reginald Jones was in the river, shouldn't I have tried harder to see if he needed help? Oh, Lordy, maybe I could have helped.

I coughed so hard my body shook and I had to lean against a lamp post. How did it feel to tumble to the bottom of a river, gallons of water pressing you down? I couldn't think of it. It was too late now to help.

I worked my route, but it was hard. Every step rattled my bones. And a hundred voices filled my head: *Tell Pete about Jonesy. No, keep it to yourself. Nothing happened. You imagined it. Tell Pete . . .*

On and on they went, a new voice for every doorstep I flung a paper onto. By the time I finished, I hardly knew who I was anymore—or even *where* I was. I had no papers left, but I'd not hawked the extras. Who'd I given them to? Looking around, I got my bearings—I was a block from home.

My face was hot and my throat as dry as sandpaper. My head pounded out a symphony of drums, and my ears felt stuffed with wads of cotton. I couldn't think, but I needed to—to figure out what Bernard Peterson and Reginald Jones had been up to. I wanted to feel better. I wanted to know what to do. I wanted . . .

My empty paper web on my shoulder, I slowly covered the last block home. I was so hot with fever by the time I got there that my eyes clouded and my knees trembled. Opening the front door, I called out to Pete, who was home from his delivery job.

"I'm home!" I tried to shout. But instead, a raspy croak came from my throat, followed by a spasm of coughs. The coughing doubled me over and racked my body, tightly squeezing my chest and throat. I couldn't breathe. *Like Reginald Jones*, a voice inside whispered. *Like Reginald Jones before he died, you wicked papist.*

It must have been then that my knees gave out and I fell to the hard wooden floor.

Chapter Sixteen

Where was I?

Voices floated from somewhere in the distance. I looked around and listened. A lonely streak of sunshine cut across the room to my bed. Where was I? Was I in Baltimore? No, Pete isn't in Baltimore . . .

"Bed rest and hot liquids . . ."

"Tea all right?"

"Yes, better than coffee. Some broth would be good . . ."

"Thanks for coming by . . ."

Dr. Beckel? His office was just two blocks over. Pete had taken me there last spring when my arm had swollen up from a bee sting.

Their voices faded with the footsteps, and eventually I heard the front door creak open and slam shut. Pete's regular tread moved below and a spigot turned on, the upstairs pipes knocking and groaning from the rushing water.

I looked around. I wasn't in my bedroom, the one I usually shared with Adam. I was in the back room, the one with the two windows overlooking the yard. My bed had been moved into a corner of the room, along with a small table that used to be in the living room. Heavy blankets had been hung like curtains over the tall windows, blocking most of the light. As my eyes adjusted to the dimness, I made out the outline of a brown glass medicine bottle on the table beside me.

My head felt like a vise was squeezing it, and I felt eerily warm, wrapped in a hundred layers of wool, but there was no sweat. I tried to sit up and go to Pete, but when I tried, the room danced and spun. Sinking back onto my pillow, I fell into a half-sleep.

When my eyes fluttered open later, Pete stood over me. He held a bowl. He looked around.

"I need a chair," he said. He placed the bowl on the bedside table and left. A few seconds later, he returned with a straight-back chair from the kitchen. Positioning himself next to the bed, he picked up the bowl and spoon.

"Try to eat some of this. It's chicken soup." He held a spoonful out to me. It smelled like health itself, all warm and homey and fragrant, and it reminded me of my mother. A now-distant image wafted through my mind: Ma bent over me with a soup spoon in her hand, urging me to eat when I was sick. I missed her now, in ways I hadn't missed her since coming west.

I wanted to eat Pete's soup, but I was so weak I could barely move. When Pete saw me struggling, he brought the spoon to my lips.

Sucking in the hot broth, I nearly cried out. It was like swallowing a thousand pins, all scratching at my throat at once.

"It'll hurt for awhile," Pete said gently. "You've got a bad throat, son. Nothing to be done but rest and drink. Mrs. McGreevey next door made this soup when she heard you were sick." He fed me another spoonful, and this one went down somewhat more easily. "The doctor says we have to make sure it doesn't become rheumatic fever. That's why I moved you in here. He said you should get some fresh air outside that stuffy old bedroom."

More soup, more talk. It was the most Pete had ever talked to me. In fact, he kept up a steady monologue while feeding me.

"I never understood why you and Adam chose to share that tiny room upstairs instead of one of you using this room as your bedroom," he continued.

I wanted to answer him—I wanted to say it had been because Adam and I didn't want to be separated, so when I chose the smaller room, Adam decided to move in with me. We'd shared a room in Baltimore, he'd told Pete at the time, and we didn't want to take up too much room. Adam had winked at me, signaling that everything would be all right, because he'd look out for me still.

But I couldn't speak. I sipped at more soup.

"The light might hurt your eyes, so we're keeping it low for a while."

"What time is it?" I whispered.

"About noon." He pulled a handkerchief out and wiped my chin.

Noon? On what day? How long have I been asleep?

As if reading my mind, he said, "You fell sick yesterday. I couldn't get Dr. Beckel here until this morning." He sounded guilty, and I wanted to thank him for all he'd done for me—moving me into this room, getting the soup, taking off from work.

I had a lot more I wanted to say, too—mostly questions. I wanted to know how long I should expect to be laid up, if Adam had come by, and, mostly, if I'd only dreamt about the burglary of the Peterson jewels, and of Adam being a fugitive, and Bernard Peterson a murderer. Just the thought of him made me shiver.

"I can get you another blanket," Pete said, placing the bowl on the table. He brought a ragged coverlet from the closet and draped it over my already warm body. He started to feed me more soup, but I shook my head. As good as it was, my stomach rebelled and the soup went sour in my mouth.

"You rest now," he said, standing. Taking the bowl and spoon away, he walked to the door. "Don't worry about anything," he said before leaving. "I'll take your paper route this afternoon and let Lester know you won't be coming in tomorrow."

———◆—◆—◆———

I lay on that sick bed for a full week. As my energy returned, so did my impatience. I wanted to find out if what I thought had transpired at the river was reality or dream. The more time went by, the more unreal it seemed, and the more I hoped it was unreal. I tried talking to Pete about it one evening. I told him I'd had the strangest dream, and then I described the evening I thought Bernard Peterson had killed Reginald Jones. Surely it would have been news by now. But Pete had only smiled and told me I was on the mend. So I concluded that maybe it hadn't happened after all.

I could hardly wait to get out of that house and return to Adam's case. I now just wanted to be done with it so I could be on my way back home. Esther and my friends were waiting for me. Sure, I wanted to go with Adam, but an idea, once unfathomable, was beginning to tease at the edges of my mind—maybe I wouldn't go back East with him. Maybe I'd go alone.

I couldn't go, though, until I knew Adam was cleared. "Look after your brother," Ma had said. She had been looking at me.

It bothered me that I didn't know where Adam was or what was happening. Had he gone to the church as I'd suggested, or found the money to head East without me?

The response to my letter only made things worse. While I recuperated that week, I heard from one jeweler, informing me he didn't have any sets like the one I described but would be happy to help me pick out something "suitable."

As I recovered, I came to appreciate the many kindnesses Pete performed for me. He not only delivered my newspapers every day, but did some work for Lester so the Academy wouldn't feel the need to hire someone in my place. And I know he gave up one of his Truth Society meetings because of a bad coughing spell I had one night. He told me he didn't mind, though, because he felt the campaign was going well, and he wouldn't be surprised if all those Klansmen received a big surprise on Election Day.

By Friday, though, I was ready to escape. That was the day I got a second jeweler's letter, telling me there were no ruby sets at "his establishment."

With Pete off at work, I managed to wobble out of bed and into a bath on my own. Still weak, I was sweating by the time I dressed and went downstairs. I fixed myself a cup of tea and tried to eat, but my throat was too dry to swallow any bread.

While I sipped at my tea, I looked through the week's newspapers. Pete might have delivered my route, but he didn't know I was expected to sell the extra papers every day. A stack of them sat on a chair in the corner.

There were the usual stories about President Harding and Portland politics, including a fair number of columns on the School Question.

I was about to close the last paper and get on my way when a headline caught my eye.

"BANKER'S BODY PULLED FROM WILLAMETTE," it screamed.

My breath caught, and I coughed and coughed. Tears streamed down my face as I struggled to catch my breath. Through blurred eyes, I began to read, my heart racing.

My nightmare had been real. Someone had been killed all right—but not Reginald Jones.

It was Bernard Peterson.

Bernard Peterson's body had been dragged from the river, a bullet through his chest. As I relived that awful night, sweat coated my body. My hands trembled as I gripped the newspaper. I had to lay it flat, my palms on either side, to stop from shaking.

Bernard Peterson was dead—not Reginald Jones.

Chapter Seventeen

Here I was again, exactly where I'd been nearly a week ago after running home sick, frightened that I'd witnessed a murder. Bad feelings washed over me—mostly guilt. Though I'd nothing to do with the crime, I hadn't told anyone about it, either. Was not reporting it a crime in itself? My legs felt wobbly just thinking about it. What if I was held accountable for not telling? What if I was guilty—of something? Officer Miller would arrest me, happy to have a boy named Matuski in his custody.

Even without an arrest, I would never let go of the feeling I could have done more. Poor Rose! She'd lost her older brother. I imagined her weeping at the news, her sweet face crumpled in sorrow.

I got myself a drink of water and sat down. Fever and time obscured the memory of that nightmarish night, its details as murky as the river itself. Dropping my head into my hands, I tried desperately to recall the events I'd witnessed.

Bernard Peterson had asked Reginald Jones to meet him at the water's edge. Bernard had threatened Jonesy with a gun, and accused him of . . . of things I couldn't quite remember. No, of things that didn't make sense. Of something connected with the bank. Why couldn't I recall? What was the matter with me? A man was murdered and I couldn't remember what happened? It should have been burned into me. All I remembered was that gun, glinting in the weak light, and Bernard's drunken anger. Holy Moses! What else? What else?

Bernard told Reginald to come to the shoreline and then—and then I hadn't been able to see, I'd only heard. I'd heard an indistinct argument, some scuffling, and a shot. I'd assumed Bernard had made good on his threat and killed Jonesy. I'd assumed Bernard had then driven his own car into the river, killing himself.

But I knew that hadn't been the case! I thought I'd seen Bernard driving away, in what must have been Jonesy's car—not Bernard's.

No, not Bernard—he'd been the one killed. It was Jonesy who drove away!

My face flushed, and it wasn't the fever but the fear.

Grabbing the paper, I looked at the article's byline, which indicated the story was written by none other than Vincent Briggs. He'd even thrown in something at the end of the tale about how Peterson's mother's house had been burglarized and some expensive jewels stolen. "Neither the thief nor the jewels have yet surfaced," he'd written.

Briggs was the man I had to talk to now. In scanning that week's newspapers, I didn't see a single story about Reginald Jones and his misdeeds at Portland Bank. I wondered why Briggs hadn't followed up on that.

Grabbing my hat and wrapping a scarf around my neck, I headed for the *Telegram* office.

"You, my boy, are the very person I wanted to see." Vincent Briggs stopped typing and took his cigar from his mouth as soon as he saw me approaching his desk. Twirling in his seat, he grabbed his coat and hat and stood. "C'mon, we're going for a walk."

"Wha—?!"

He grabbed me by the elbow and escorted me downstairs, through the lobby and out onto the cold street.

"You realize what trouble you're in, don't you?" Outside, he looked up and down the street, and placed the cigar back in his mouth. We waited while cars and horse-drawn carts passed.

"I didn't do it!" I protested. "I mean, I just didn't know if it was real or not. I got sick, see, and . . ."

Briggs led me up the street to a sandwich shop. Inside, he took me to a back booth, frequently glancing over his shoulder, as if he expected the cops to pounce on us any second. On a normal day, the shop, with its black-and-white-tiled floor and wooden booths, was bright and comfortable, especially with the aroma of chicken soup, which I could smell even through my stuffed nose. When a cheerful serving girl came over for our order, Briggs barked out, "Two coffees. And an ice cream for him. Chocolate."

After she'd gone, Briggs tapped the table with his cigar-laden hand. "You were seen at the bank talking to Peterson the day of the murder," he said in a hushed voice.

My mouth dropped open and I stopped breathing.

"Oh, they haven't figured out it was you. They said it was some kid named Miller." Briggs leaned his head back and gave out a hearty laugh. "Nice touch, son, using the good officer's last name."

"I . . . I . . . is that a crime?" I asked feebly.

Vincent shrugged. "If I were you, I'd worry about crimes more serious than just using an officer's last name to play some game of detective."

When I stared at him silently, he continued. "From the teller's description, I knew it was you," he said. "And then the cops said they'd found a rosary at the scene of the crime. You wouldn't happen to be missing one, would you?" He stared at me through dark, skeptical slits, following my hand as I slowly inched it into my coat pocket, searching, searching . . . My mother's rosary! I must have dropped it that night. And then, when I'd fallen ill, I hadn't thought to check if it was still with me.

Briggs frowned, as if sad to discover he was right. He lapsed into silence as the serving girl came by with our coffees and my ice cream. But I couldn't eat it now. I had no appetite.

Briggs took a noisy sip of coffee and stared at me. "Don't you see, boy? Bernard Peterson's dead. Your brother's been targeted for stealing his mother's heirloom jewelry. You were seen talking to Bernard Peterson the day he went in the river. And now there's evidence you were at the scene of the crime . . ."

"Holy—" My eyes went wide, and I saw myself in the future, prison-garbed, being led to the gallows.

"*Holy* is right, kid. This mess is going to get all tied up with local politics. 'BOY KILLS BROTHER'S ACCUSER.' And the rosary—Lordy, it's as if you were crying out for the Klan to rally around this one. They'll make the Peterson family victims of a Polish Catholic gang of murdering thieves—'the very thing Oregon needs to rid itself of. So vote for the School Question, folks, and make sure we don't produce any more of these anti-American Bolshevik killers!'" He pounded the table.

"I didn't do it," I said quietly.

He sucked on his dead cigar. "I didn't figure you did. Somehow, I don't see shooting a fellow through the heart as part of your repertoire."

"I didn't do it," I repeated as if he hadn't heard. "But I know who did."

Vincent Briggs kept me in that sandwich shop for an hour, prodding me for every detail I could remember. My ice cream melted and he ordered me some soup when he realized I was really sick. While I ate, he pulled out a small notebook and pencil and wrote as I talked.

I told him about the bank conversation, as much as I could remember, and how I "stole" a ride on Peterson's Model T. I told him about Reginald Jones, the argument, and the sounds that convinced me Peterson had killed Jonesy, not the other way around.

"All right," he said, flipping back through his pages, "what else you remember about Peterson? You said he got upset when you asked to see Jones?"

"Yeah, real nervous. But so was the teller. They didn't want to talk about him. That's when I made up the name," I reminded him. "I didn't realize there'd be a real Mary Miller in their records."

"Well, it's a pretty common name," said Briggs. "But go on. Anything you can remember, tell me. What else did he say? 'He asked about her account, said he'd fix it'?" he read from his notes.

"He asked if it had been a loan. And then, when he found her records, he kept telling me not to worry, he'd fix it, the bank had made a mistake and sent her some bills she shouldn't have gotten." I hoped that was what he'd said. It was hard to remember after being in bed with a fever all week.

Briggs tapped the notebook with his pencil. "A loan . . . are you sure you didn't mention it was a loan you were coming to see Jones about?"

I shook my head. "I'm sure. I don't know anything about banking except savings accounts and stuff."

"Did Jones work in loans?" he asked, more of himself than of me.

"When he talked to Jonesy at the river, he mentioned loans,"

I said. Quietly, I added, "And he said he knew it would come to this—getting rid of Jonesy, that is."

"But Jones was getting money from Peterson, right?" Briggs looked at his notes again.

"Yeah, Peterson said something about paying Jonesy. And then when Jonesy saw Peterson had a gun . . . he said Peterson didn't have to pay anymore."

"It sounds like Reginald Jones was blackmailing Bernard Peterson." He chewed on his cigar and didn't say anything for a few seconds.

I finished my soup and sipped at some coffee. "Why didn't you ever write the story about Jonesy?" I asked after a while.

Vincent Briggs snapped his gaze back toward me and blinked. "Oh, that. I made a call to the bank. They said he'd left for another job. Didn't seem like anything."

"But Peterson said something about him taking cash from the bank," I said in a hushed, excited voice. "And that's what my brother and his friend told me, too—that Jonesy was in trouble because he was stealing or something."

Briggs's mouth lifted into a faint smile. "Hmmm . . . guess that gives me two sources. I could always squeeze the bank president with that." He rubbed his chin reflectively.

"What do you mean?" I asked.

"Well, I call the bank president, see? And I tell him I have two separate people who are willing to go on the record saying Reginald Jones was let go because he was stealing. And if he won't comment on it, I'll just print that he refused to comment. And it looks bad for him and the bank." He smiled broadly now. "Right about then, they usually find something to say." But his smile faded. "Still, the best thing for both of us is to find Reginald Jones."

"Why 'for both of us'?" I asked. A quiver of fear shot through my spine.

Briggs's voice was serious and sad. "Like I said before," he said, "once they figure out it was you in that field by the river, they won't look any further. You've got the wrong last name, the wrong religion, and the wrong amount of evidence pointing your way. It won't matter that you didn't do it." He studied me, his brow creased and his long mouth pressed into an unhappy frown.

I did know what he meant, and I told him about the cross-burning in front of Pete's house. He sighed heavily, then reached over to tap me gently on the arm.

"'This too shall pass,'" he said softly. His frown lifted into a faint smile. "They'll find another group soon enough to pin the world's problems on. And your kind will be off the hook."

That gave me little comfort. *I* wouldn't be "off the hook" until I solved this problem, the one that had started with the jewel theft. I'd certainly bungled that investigation so far. I'd spent so much time following up the Jonesy lead that I'd neglected others, like the Petersons' servants. Maybe they knew something. Maybe they were responsible for the theft in the first place. I looked up at Briggs.

"Do you know how I can find out where the Peterson servants live?" I asked.

A weak smile again played on his face. "Always searching, aren't you?" He shook his head. "I looked into their servants. They're good people, never in trouble, no debts, and well-paid. They'd hardly have cause to steal from their employers when they're treated so well. And they won't say a bad word about anyone in the family. Believe me, I tried to get them to."

Another possibility gone.

He looked at his watch. "I have to go, kid." After dropping some money on the table, he stood. "Don't forget—finding Reginald Jones helps us both." He peeled off a few more dollars from his billfold and slid them toward me. "Buy your uncle a nice steak or something. Tell him it's a bonus for your good newspaper work." With a quick wink and a pat on my shoulder, he left.

———◆◆◆◆———

After my meeting with Briggs, I was sure I'd be snatched off the street by every passing police officer. Even a dour-looking man glancing my way sent me scurrying into the shadows. I felt like a marked man, wanted for a crime I didn't commit. But, in a way, maybe I had committed it. I didn't stop it. No wonder Adam had been so reluctant to pursue the real thief. If you're wanted by the law for something you didn't do, you feel like running—especially when you think nobody will believe you, and especially when part of you feels guilty about something. Now his resistance to drawing attention to himself, his reluctance to pursue the case, to lie low instead, all made sense. I felt stupid as well as sad. But I had no choice. I had to keep pushing forward and solve the case or end up in worse trouble myself.

My walk home was slow and roundabout, to avoid as many of Officer Miller's usual haunts as possible. By the time I arrived, I was too tired to do anything but go up to bed, so I hid the money Briggs had given me under my mattress and fell asleep, still dressed.

When I woke up, I could tell the day's light was fading and I heard Pete rattling around in the kitchen downstairs. Yawning, I walked down to talk to him. He stirred a big pot on the stove that smelled as good as the soup from the sandwich shop.

"Fish chowder," Pete said, smiling. "It'll be good for you."

Fish—it was Friday, and I'd forgotten! I'd eaten chicken soup at the sandwich shop! A pang of guilt pinched my heart. It seemed like nothing good had happened to me lately.

A few minutes later, as we ate our chowder together, Pete asked me how I was feeling. I told him I was just fine, and we continued on in silence.

"You miss your brother, don't you?" he asked softly.

"I guess so," I said without looking at him. I wondered if he'd seen Adam or knew what had become of him.

"Let's hope and pray he finds his way," Pete said. "I light a candle for him at church."

"What do you mean?"

"If he's guilty, he should make things right," he said slowly.

"He's not guilty," I said. But my usual forcefulness was gone. My illness, Bernard Peterson's death, and the anti-Catholic feelings running so strong all around me—they had worn me down, and I couldn't muster the righteous indignation I usually felt when someone accused Adam. I just wanted everything to be fixed. Besides, anything I said would only make matters worse. If I told Pete that I now knew how Adam felt, I'd have to tell him of the crime I could soon be accused of. I didn't want to cause Pete any more trouble. If I did have to go the police, I'd do it like a man, on my own.

After dinner, I offered to help clean up, but Pete told me to rest. I dragged myself upstairs and lay on my bed, but after my evening nap, sleep wouldn't come.

I thought of Ma, and Adam and Pete, and that burning cross on our lawn. I thought of the people who'd hang the charge of murder on me once they found out I had been at the river the night Bernard Peterson was killed.

The world was a horrible place. I could be branded a murderer! There were lots of people—angry, anonymous people—who thought bad things about me without even knowing who I was. They wanted to believe both Adam and I were bad, and they wanted us locked away . . . or worse. Sweat coated my body, both from fever and fear. I wanted it all to go away.

Most of all, I wanted to go home to Baltimore and thought, for a few minutes, of simply running away. But no—no, I wouldn't do that. I wouldn't follow Adam's lead.

Eventually, I fell asleep. When I awoke, darkness covered the room, the only light, from a silvery moon high in the chalky sky, flooding my room with gray shadows. A fever must have broken while I'd slept, because my body was slick with sweat, but it cooled me and calmed me.

"Find Reginald Jones." That's what Vincent Briggs had said to do. I'd done a lot already: enlisted Briggs to help, and learned about Reginald and Bernard.

But I was so tired. Not just physically tired, but exhausted on the inside. I now understood how Adam had felt—like he was pushing a big boulder up a steep cliff, with folks above him waiting to kick it back down again—folks like Officer Miller, calling him "papist," "Bolshevik."

But there was nothing I could do about the way the world looked at us. I could only muster the energy to fix the one problem that threatened my future and Adam's. Whether I wanted to or not, I had to find Reginald Jones.

Where would he have gone after the incident at the waterfront? Lillian had said he came from a good family, and didn't need the bank job. If that was true, his family could afford to hide him, or to send him away. But he had been around that night at the river, even well after being fired. So maybe he was still around now.

One other piece of the puzzle didn't fit. Why would rich people need money? If Reginald Jones's family had money, why had Jonesy stolen from the bank? Maybe if I answered that question, I could figure out the rest.

If Reginald Jones was desperate enough to steal from the bank, he might well be desperate enough to steal from a fellow worker's house. He could have swiped the jewels. Finding him was crucial for both Adam and me.

I knew only one place to look—the speakeasy I'd followed Adam to. I'd have to go there on my own, and with Pete asleep, I had to go *now*.

Holding my shoes, I crept downstairs in stocking feet so as not to wake Pete. When the cool night air hit my face, I breathed in deeply, feeling determined again—driven and on the hunt.

Still, on the street, I kept looking over my shoulder. My back felt prickly, as if someone were behind me. There weren't many strangers around at that hour, but I imagined every one wearing a white hood and sheet. Everyone was a potential enemy. And police—the people I used to think of as protectors—I now viewed as thieves, ready to steal away my freedom without a second thought. I had only a narrow road to traverse, with danger on both sides, and I didn't dare slip or go off course.

Arriving at the speakeasy, I breathed deep and used the special knock. Once inside, I heard the sound of loud jazz music and glistening laughter from the back room.

"I'm looking for Lillian," I shouted over the din to the dark-eyed woman who'd let me in.

"She's in the back," she purred. "With her boyfriend."

Finding my way, I looked around the dark, smoky room, adjusting to the dimness. There she was, over in a corner, leaning into the table and talking, her face a bright oval of good cheer.

And across from her was a familiar sight—my brother, Adam.

Chapter Eighteen

When I saw my brother in that speakeasy, relief and anger fought each other for control, and anger won out. In the speakeasy again? Would he never learn? The times I'd thought of him running and hiding, I'd also thought he'd improve his life, maybe find some decent work—start a new life while he waited for me to clear his name. But here he was, back to his old ways, at risk of being caught and doing nothing to better the situation.

As I strode toward his table, he spotted me. He didn't smile, instead pulling his chair back an inch as if about to run away—from me, his own brother!

"What are you doing here?" I asked, standing in front of him and Lillian.

"I'm having fun," he said in a surly tone. "It's the one thing I know how to do."

Lillian glanced at him with sadness in her eyes, then gestured to the seat next to her. "Join us," she said.

But I tugged at Adam's shoulder. "Get up and get out of here."

"Hey!" He shrugged away from me and swiped his shoulder where I'd touched him.

I wouldn't be dusted off or shoved away! I grabbed the scruff of his jacket and pulled him to his feet. My fists clenched and I was ready to punch him, but before I had a chance to swing, big hands clamped on my shoulders. The strong man I'd seen the first time I was here dragged me away.

"We don't like trouble," the man growled as he pulled me toward the door.

"Adam, say something!" Lillian said, looking from me to my brother and back again. "He's your brother, isn't he?"

Adam breathed out an irritated sigh. "He didn't mean any harm," he said at last. "Let him go."

The man stopped at the door, paused, and pushed me away. I nearly stumbled to the floor, catching my balance by grabbing a table and knocking over a glass of whiskey. A man sputtered a curse, but I moved away and back toward Adam.

Adam gestured to an empty chair near Lillian and I sat down.

I didn't waste my time asking how Adam was faring. The whiskey bottle and a deck of cards on the table told the tale. He was drinking, he was carousing, and he wasn't doing a darn thing to help his cause. I was on my own.

All right. I'd do it. I'd come here for a reason, and it wasn't to fight my brother.

"I need to find Reginald Jones fast," I announced, looking from Adam to Lillian. Quickly, I explained the situation—the whole of it. If I didn't find Jonesy, I couldn't prove I wasn't the man who'd killed Bernard Peterson.

"Did you try—" Lillian started to say, but Adam interrupted her.

"Leave it alone, Carl," Adam said to me.

"What?" I stared at my brother, unbelieving. Lillian seemed to know where Jonesy might be. Why wouldn't Adam let her tell me?

"Why did Jonesy need money? Why was he stealing?" I said.

"Gambling," Lillian said before Adam could stop her. Her lower lip stuck out in a pout. "That gambling ring by the waterfront. You know 'em, Adam. They're the ones who—"

"Shut up, Lil!" Adam's faced reddened and Lillian cringed, as if she'd been slapped. I stared at Adam. Telling a girl to "shut up"? We hadn't been raised that way.

"Tell me about the gambling ring," I said to Lillian.

Giving up, Adam slumped back in his chair as Lillian folded her hands in front of her and answered. "It's run by some fellow from San Francisco. He has his own club on the north side," she said. "We used to go there. Good music. Good booze. And craps and poker. Some other games, too. What were they, Adam?" She looked at him but he didn't answer, so she continued. "They were real nice at first. If you lost money, they loaned some to you—said you could pay it off with your winnings later."

Adam snorted with disgust and spoke up. "Yeah, 'later.'"

"But then they got real mean if you didn't pay up. And they set up these payments that were just awful. Lots of extra cash—interest—on your loan. Adam had to pay some off."

Adam didn't look at me.

"Is that what you used my money for?" I asked Adam, my voice rising. "You didn't gamble with it. You paid off old gambling debts!"

He scowled and didn't answer.

"Most of them," said Lillian.

Knowing I wouldn't get the truth from Adam, I continued, to Lillian, "So Jonesy was in debt to these fellows. Where are they?"

"They shut down," Lillian said.

"At least the gambling part," my brother added.

"What do you mean?" I asked.

Lillian shuddered. "They only do the enforcement now—the loan enforcement."

"If you don't pay, they make life real uncomfortable for you," Adam said.

"They hurt people," Lillian explained. "They cut off Billy Ramone's little finger." Shivering, she ran her hands up her arms. "I can't think about it."

That would certainly explain why Jonesy, if he were a poor man, would steal to pay off his gambling debts. But he was rich. And these loans—were these the loans Bernard Peterson was so concerned about? And what did they have to do with the bank?

"Why didn't Jonesy just get the cash from his family?" I asked.

"He did—part of it," Adam told me. "But his father said he had to earn the rest of the money himself. They didn't understand what these guys were like. They thought if Jonesy just treated it like an ordinary debt . . ."

". . . he wouldn't be hurt," Lillian finished.

"Where is he now?" I asked, again looking from one to the other.

Adam remained silent while Lillian fidgeted in her chair. She knew something. They both did. Yet Adam wouldn't tell me. He wouldn't help me, even though it could clear my name, and even though I'd been working so hard to clear his. He was as bad as the rest—as bad as Officer Miller. Adam wouldn't put me away, but he wouldn't help me, either.

Then I thought—had Adam been gambling in Baltimore? Is that why we had to leave? Is that what Esther had meant in her letter when she'd wondered where Adam was? Did she know he was a troublemaker, that he had to escape his debts? *Crap*. I couldn't even think about that now. That Adam would steal my home from me . . . No, it couldn't be. All this time, all this longing for home . . .

Over the past few weeks, I'd come to the sad realization that my brother had stopped being a good person. Now, I had to take in another painful lesson—he'd stopped being a good brother, too. No, worse than that—maybe he'd never been the good person or the good brother I'd imagined. Maybe he'd always been like this but I hadn't seen.

I could barely look at him. But I had to.

"Adam," I pleaded, "if I don't find him, the police might come after me!"

He let out a cynical bark of a laugh. "They'll come after you anyway. The whole Klan'll be after you, just like they were after me. They'll say you shot down a pillar of Portland society, a good Christian boy, not a mongrel like us. You could have had Jesus Christ himself as witness and it wouldn't matter. Take my advice, Carl. Get out of town . . . and quick."

Stunned, I sat back. My head began to throb from the steady beat of the jazz drummer, the cigarette smoke, and the lingering effects of my illness. I gave up on Adam and looked at Lillian, whose mouth opened as if she was about to speak.

"Please," I said, "tell me where you think he might be."

A sharp glance from Adam silenced her.

———— ❖ ————

I didn't stay much longer—just long enough to learn that Adam was hiding out at Lillian's place. She rented a room in a boarding house not too far from the speakeasy. During the day, she worked at a ladies' dress shop near Meier and Frank's. Adam stayed in the room while she worked, and it sounded like they went out a lot at night, looking for good times or poker games where Adam could try to win some cash to pay off his debts. I got the impression Lillian thought they'd get married someday. Adam didn't say much during that part of the discussion.

It was nearly midnight when I left them. By then, fatigue had folded over me like a wet blanket. Before I left, I looked at Adam and wanted to ask him why he wouldn't help me. I wanted to say goodbye. But all I did was nod my head at him, as if nothing had changed and I'd see him at home soon.

In the cool night air, I looked up and down the street, wondering where Reginald Jones could be if he was still in the city. His family was well-to-do, so he probably lived near the Petersons, or maybe in Vincent Briggs's neighborhood. Maybe if I kept a lookout by the Briggs house, I'd see him coming and going. But I was far too tired for that—too tired and wrung out.

As I took my first step toward home, a voice whispered from the porch of the speakeasy.

"Pssst! Carl!" It was Lillian. Turning, I saw her standing alone, holding a flimsy silk purse in front of her and glancing over her shoulder. I went to her.

"Adam's paying our tab," she explained, then looked down with an embarrassed grimace. "Well, he's paying, but I gave him the money." A door opened inside the speakeasy and she glanced over her shoulder. Speaking fast, she said, "Look, Jonesy might have left town. But he might be at a house on Third. His father owns it and it's empty. You could look there."

Third Street! That was the house Adam had hidden in weeks before. Of course—Adam must have learned about it from Jonesy!

"Thanks, Lillian. Thanks so much." I touched my hat and ran off into the night, turning left at the end of the empty road, heading southeast toward the abandoned house on Third.

I no longer felt tired.

Although I was still a little weak, I couldn't stop. If Jonesy hadn't hit the road already, he'd surely do so soon. After all, he'd killed a man.

As I ran down the dark, empty streets, I thought about the night of the killing. There had been an argument and a scuffle. I'd heard but not seen it. And Bernard Peterson had been slightly drunk. Jonesy hadn't shown up at that meeting intending to do harm, but Bernard had. It was now clear to me what had happened—Jonesy had grabbed the gun in their fight and killed Bernard in self-defense.

If I could convince him to talk to the police, he could get off. He came from a good family and had a good name. He wasn't Catholic—I was. And I could be heading to the gallows if Jonesy didn't come forward.

A block from the house, my breath caught and I started to cough. Stopping, I bent over and sucked in air. That only made it worse. Coughing consumed my whole body, shaking me to the core. My ears rang and head throbbed while I barked into the night like a wounded dog. Gasps of air kept me from passing out, but each intake only fed the sickness. Holding onto a lamp post for balance, I gagged and choked. To a passer-by, I must have looked like a drunk at the end of a bad binge. I thought I was going to die.

At last, as tears streamed down my face, the coughing stopped. Sucking in a slow, tentative breath, I waited. No cough—it was gone. I could breathe. Wiping my mouth, I felt dark and strangled.

Walking slowly now, I wondered if I should just turn around and forget about everything. Maybe Adam was right. Maybe it wasn't worth it. Maybe I should collect my next paper route paycheck and head back home to Baltimore. If I didn't have enough money for train fare, I could jump a train and ride for free in a freight car. I'd seen some hoboes doing that on our way to Portland.

I saw myself in a small row home in Baltimore like the one we'd left, coming home from a hard day at a nearby factory. I saw Esther there, waiting for me, smiling over a steaming pot, asking me how my day had been.

But before I could enjoy this dream, memory intruded. Again, I saw my mother telling *me*—yes, me, not Adam—to "look after" my brother. She'd seen what I hadn't, that Adam was weak, that he needed someone to watch over him. She hadn't feared for my future, but for his. I couldn't go home to Baltimore until I saw to both our futures.

I stood before the "hideout" house—dark and still, looming above, and shutting all intruders out. I saw no evidence of life. What was I thinking? Jonesy would be crazy to hang around town after what he'd done. He was probably long gone. He wasn't stupid. Unlike me, he wasn't trying to fight injustices and right wrongs, looking and hoping for the best in everyone. I felt another cough tickle my throat. Soon I'd be bent over, gagging again and raising the alarm for blocks. *Darn it.*

Turning, I coughed softly into the shadows. Swallowing hard to control my hacking, I bent forward. A sliver of light flickered above. Whipping my head up, I saw a glow behind the shade in the room my brother had stayed in. Jonesy hadn't left town. He was still here after all.

Chapter Nineteen

Sometimes, bad things can turn into good ones. If I'd arrived at the house a few minutes earlier, I might have knocked, gotten no answer, given up, and gone on my way, never seeing the light upstairs. But because I'd been delayed by my coughing fit, I now knew Jonesy was here, whether he'd answer the door or not.

But now what? Somehow, I didn't think he'd be impressed by a fifteen-year-old "kid." If only Vincent Briggs was with me. I could see the tough reporter in my mind, persuading Jonesy to tell the true story. *Come on, boy, I know you didn't mean to do it. Better to tell me than the police, right? They'd be ashamed to arrest you after all of Portland reads the truth about Bernard Peterson.*

Vincent Briggs was self-confident and smart. He'd probably fit in anywhere. No wonder he could get people to tell him their deepest secrets. He could be strong and intimidating, or warm and kind, whichever would work best. I couldn't imagine him ever feeling the doubt I felt in that bank, or at the train station—as if everybody else knew what they were doing but me.

I wished he was here with me, or at least I wished I could ask him how to do his job, but he wasn't here. I had only myself. And I had Reginald Jones nearly in my grasp. I couldn't walk away now—I'd worked too hard and come too far.

I patted my pocket and found some of the "Sister Lucretia"

posters I'd crammed in there the other day. I folded them over so only the blank sides showed. I didn't have a pencil on me, but I'd borrow one. After smoothing my sweaty hair under my cap, I strode toward the door and pulled myself up. Then I knocked, using the special speakeasy pattern—the one I'd used with Adam when he'd hidden here.

I heard a rustling above and then the light went out. I knocked again. In a forceful voice, I called out, "Reginald Jones, open up. It's Carl Matuski from the *Telegram*." I knocked again. Still no answer.

What had Briggs said in the sandwich shop? He'd said he could use the information I provided to "squeeze" the truth out of the bank officers. Maybe I could do the same.

"Listen, Jonesy," I said, "we already know what happened. It was an accident. We know Bernard Peterson was trying to kill you that night." I deepened my voice. "He was stealing from the bank and you knew about it. You were going to tell the bank and he tried to stop you. If you don't talk to us, the police will think you killed him in cold blood."

Seconds passed. Would he come? Finally, a shuffling gait grew louder and closer. The door creaked open and I was staring Reginald Jones in the face.

What a sight he was! Several scratches marked his right cheek, and his right eye was swollen and bruised. His dark hair was unevenly cut, with a patch near his forehead shaven close to his skull, revealing a crusted scrape. His long face looked permanently set in a scowl, with thin lips drooping downward and the swollen eye half-shut.

"You're kind of young to work for the *Telegram*," he whispered, looking over my shoulder to make sure I was alone. "You Adam's brother?"

Affecting a self-assurance I barely felt, I said, "Yeah. That's what got me interested in all this. I work with Vincent Briggs, the *Telegram*'s top reporter. Me and Vinnie are real close."

Jonesy, staring hard at me, said nothing. His hand still gripped the door and it was clear he was considering shutting me out.

"Talk to me," I said quickly. "Tell me your story. You deserve to have your side told."

Through narrowed eyes, he looked me up and down. One hand was hidden behind the door—I wondered if it held a weapon. Should I run? Was I in danger? After all, Reginald Jones had killed a man. He might want to get rid of anyone who knew.

I didn't care anymore. I stood my ground and waited, daring him to throw me out. This plan *had* to work.

"You don't look good," I said in a soothing tone. "You need to sit down. C'mon, let's go upstairs and talk." I pointed at the steps.

"I'm tired," he said to no one. "I'm just tired."

Jonesy turned and walked up, and I followed close behind. He limped, his right leg straight and unbending.

"Bernie beat you up pretty good, I see," I said in a friendly voice.

"I'm not well," he muttered, again to himself more than to me. "I'm sick." He sounded like he was whimpering.

"He must have hurt you bad," I offered, hoping to keep him talking. We were near the second floor now.

"Kicked me in the shins." Surprise colored his voice. The beating still stung him.

Upstairs, I followed him into the front bedroom. The only furnishings were a mattress and lamp on the floor and a small table and chair along the wall. He eased himself onto the mattress. I took the chair.

"How do I know you'll help me?" he asked, rubbing his sore right leg.

"I don't help anyone but the truth," I said, repeating a line Vincent Briggs had used on me. It sounded hollow in my voice, though, so I cleared my throat and tried again. "And the truth is Bernard Peterson tried to kill you."

"That's it," he whispered, his eyes wide, his voice absent.

"You just need to tell me the details," I said. He was so disoriented I was afraid he wouldn't be able to tell me anything worthwhile. I had to keep him focused and on track. "What do you remember?"

"I'm not staying here long," he said, "so if you want the story, you better get it quick."

The story—I pulled out my piece of paper and let out a pretend chuckle. "Forgot my pencil. Got one?"

Jonesy didn't flinch. He grabbed a jacket from the end of the mattress and fished a pencil from it. After tossing it to me, he sucked in his breath.

"Let's start at the beginning," I said, my mind racing. What exactly was the beginning when a reporter covered a story? Were there rules to this job? Was there a "first question" I should ask? Before I had a chance to formulate one, Jonesy spoke.

"It was an accident," he said in a small, high-pitched, quivering voice. He sounded miserable. "The gun went off accidentally. I didn't mean to shoot him. I just didn't want him to shoot me. He said he had to get rid of me, that he couldn't risk what I'd say or do. He said he'd been thinking about how to do it for a long time . . . He wasn't right in the head . . ." He didn't look at me when he talked, and kept rubbing his leg.

I wrote everything down quickly, exactly as he'd said it.

"Peterson was doing something wrong at the bank," I began.

He looked at me eagerly. "Yes," he said, "embezzling. Bernie needed a lot of cash . . ."

". . . to pay off the gambling ring," I said.

Nodding, he continued, "And, just like me, he couldn't borrow any more from his father. If he'd known how much he owed, his father would have disowned him. So Bernie came up with this plan . . ."

"Involving loans . . ." I scribbled furiously, unsure if my writings would be worth anything later, but it was the only way to keep Jonesy talking.

"Yes, he'd fill out these phony loan applications, making up names. He only did a few, but it was enough to raise the money he needed."

"Didn't the bank wonder when nobody paid off the loans?"

"The bank would call a loan if somebody missed three payments. But if the loan officer—Bernie in this case—made special arrangements, more payments could be missed."

"Wouldn't the bank catch on eventually?" My pencil hovered over the paper.

"Sure, but Bernie figured he'd have the cash by then to pay the bank. He was desperate for money, though, because of—"

"The gang," I finished. "I know about Billy Ramone's finger."

Jonesy nodded. "They're pitiless, cold-hearted—" He didn't finish that thought. "And they find you no matter where you hide. You're never safe." He looked up at the ceiling. "Why'd I ever get involved with them?"

"About Bernie," I said, drawing him back to the story. "How was he going to keep the bank from knowing? Was he going to leave town? Get money from somewhere else?" *From pawning family jewels?* I wondered.

"He was going to get an inheritance, he said—from his father-in-law. The fellow passed away a couple months ago, and they were just waiting for the will to be settled. But it was taking too long, so Bernie had to act."

Or maybe the inheritance story was a sham and selling the

jewels was the real windfall he'd been waiting for. At last, I felt my hunches were paying off. Rose's brother had been in on it all along. I couldn't wait to tell Adam, however mad I was at him.

"But you knew what he'd done," I said more to myself than to Jonesy. That's why Jonesy blackmailed Bernie. He knew about the bank loan scheme.

"I was going to do the right thing. Honest! I wasn't going to ask Bernie for any more cash!" He reached for his jacket, pulling it to him. "But Bernie—he was wild that night. Just crazy. He was swinging that gun in my face and threatening to kill me. He was going to dump my body in the river! He told me how he'd planned it! I couldn't just let him shoot me and walk away! I had to fight. I . . ."

Jonesy then pulled something from the pocket of his jacket, and I swallowed, hard.

There, in the palm of his hand, was the gun.

Chapter Twenty

As Jonesy talked, holding the gun, my pencil froze over the paper. He was beginning to sound as crazy as Bernard Peterson had that night by the river. His voice was squeaky and trembling. His hands shook as he gestured. His eyes were wide and wild. I had to calm him down, get the rest of the story, and keep him from leaving town. In what I hoped was a soothing voice, I said to him, "That's evidence, Jonesy. Best not to touch it. It's probably got Bernie's fingerprints all over it, right?"

The gun lay flat in the palm of his hand. Staring at it, he said, "That's right—his fingerprints. He was waving it at me like a madman!"

I pulled from my pocket a clean handkerchief, the one I'd made sure to keep on me after my lunch with Rose, and handed it to him. "Here, wrap it in this. It can clear your name, Jonesy. It'll prove your story."

Like a child, he looked up at me, and for a breathtaking second, I wondered if he'd hand over the gun or use it—on me or himself.

The room was still except for the sound of our breathing. He lifted the gun up, his fingers caressing its steely handle, his index finger sliding toward the trigger. My eyes began to close, waiting for him to pull that trigger, ending either my life or his.

As he fingered the weapon, his eyes took on a glazed look. His mind was far away, having perhaps returned to that night he'd shot Bernard Peterson. He'd killed one man. Would it be easier now to kill again? Bile rose in my throat. I swallowed, and the effort unleashed another coughing jag.

Bringing my hand to my mouth, I dropped the handkerchief and hacked away for a full minute, my face reddening as I struggled for air.

It was enough to shift the mood. Jonesy turned to me, his brow furrowed with concern. Laying the gun on the handkerchief in front of me, he stood and started patting me on the back to ease the coughing. "You're sick, too," he said.

"Yeah," I managed between coughs. Once the fit passed, I quickly scooped up the gun in its cloth cover. "It's getting better now," I said hoarsely. "Now, tell me about that night."

Rubbing his head, he settled back on the mattress.

"It was an awful fight and I was never good at fighting. I can't even remember getting into a fight, except maybe with my brother when we were kids. But Bernie, he was treating it like it was a game, like we were wrestling in school. He was laughing and shouting, but he wouldn't let go of the gun. He punched me and scraped me. But he wouldn't let go of the gun!"

His voice went high and quivering again. "He just wouldn't. I tried to reason with him. When he started laughing, I said, 'Bernie, come on, this is ridiculous.' And he jammed it in my chest. I thought I'd be dead in a single click!" He paused, blinking fast. "So I rammed into him as fast and hard as I could, grabbed that gun, and twisted his hand . . . oh, dear Lord . . ."

He bent over and sobbed.

"And then the gun went off," I said softly into the quiet room. He wasn't listening. He was lost in his misery. It filled the room, touching me, too, as I imagined the awful scene. I again smelled the river that night, and heard the cawing gulls, the lap of the water, and the shuffling of the two men as they struggled. It was horrible for me to remember. What must it have been like for him?

When he'd regained control, he said, "I didn't know what to do. I pocketed the gun. I was going to leave. And then, and then . . . I realized I couldn't just leave him there. I dragged his body to the river and dumped it in. Then I had the idea of driving his car in as well. I thought maybe they'd think it was a car accident, that they wouldn't notice the gunshot wound when they found him. I didn't think they'd find him so fast." His shoulders shook as he cried.

Not knowing what else to do, I wrote it all down, word for word, while he cried it out.

"Now I'm a murderer," he said, "as well as a thief."

"You're not a murderer," I told him. "You killed Bernard Peterson because he was going to kill you."

"Is that how you'll write it up?" he asked eagerly.

Folding the paper, I stood. "I'll do better than that. I'll get our best reporter to write it up himself. But you have to come with me. Now."

* * *

Despite his addled state, it didn't take much convincing to get him to go with me to Briggs's house. In fact, he led me to his car, hidden behind the house, and drove us there. His confession loosened his tongue even more, so he spent the lonely drive giving me more details about Bernard Peterson's death. I scribbled them down as best I could in the dark.

When we arrived at Vincent Briggs's house, I thought fast and rushed to the front door. Banging on it, I shouted out his name.

"Vinnie, Vinnie!" I yelled at the windows on the second floor. "It's Carl, your *assistant*." After rousing Briggs from a good night's sleep, I barreled into my story as we stood on the front step, telling him in a deep, serious tone how I, his trusty assistant, had "gotten the story"—just as he'd instructed me to—and how now we'd beat *The Daily Oregonian* to it.

Dressed in a dark-red velvet robe and sleeping cap, Briggs glared at me but played along, leading us into his dark study. Once there, he listened as I blurted out the facts as Jonesy had told them to me.

Leaning into his desk, his chin in his hand, he asked me for my "notes." I handed over the sheets with my scribblings, swelling with pride when I saw his face change from amusement to admiration.

"Good work, Carl. Very good work," he said in a voice that was straight and sincere. He had a few more questions of his own, of course, and I listened, rapt, as he got Jonesy to talk about the blackmail in a way that didn't make him uncomfortable admitting to it. I saw Briggs writing fast and using funny abbreviations and shortcuts for words so he could get it all down. I would ask him about those later.

At the end of the session, Jonesy pulled the gun from his jacket, causing Briggs's eyes to bug out of his head.

"Well, well," he said, looking at it, "that should clear everything up. Give it to me, son, and be on your way. I won't tell the police where you are because I don't know. But once my story appears, I expect you'll be safe coming out of your hiding place."

With a look of immense gratitude, Reginald Jones limped out the door. Before I left, Vincent Briggs patted me on the shoulder and held me back.

"You could have a future in the newspaper trade, young man.

Good work."

—•◦••◦•—

That Tuesday, the big story in all the newspapers was about a huge Klan rally at an old farm south of town. Several thousand Klansmen gathered to welcome several hundred new recruits into the fold. Instead of a flaming cross, the article said, they used a big electric one. *Huh? An electric one?* Guess all you had to do to the electric one was unplug it. There were speeches about "keeping America American," and the "threat of the mongrel Communists from across the seas whose names as well as religion make them unfit to enjoy the privileges of this great country."

Even with that story and the related School Question taking up the front page, Vincent Briggs still managed to snag the lower right corner with his article. "BANK EMBEZZLEMENT LEADS TO DEATH," it was headlined. I was surprised to read at the end of it that Reginald Jones had turned himself in for the death of Bernard Peterson, but no charges were likely to be filed. It was a clear-cut case of self-defense. But the alleged blackmail was another matter, and Jonesy's lawyers were "talking with the D.A."

Because of the story, I relaxed a bit that week. My body was still weak, though, and more than once I had to leave a room because of a coughing fit. I was only working half of what I was supposed to for Lester, but he didn't complain. Pete wanted the doctor to look me over again, but I knew we couldn't afford it, so I told him I was fine.

The Wednesday after the story appeared, I started delivering my papers again, and Officer Miller was once again waiting for me.

"Seen your brother around?" he asked. His voice—had it been one of those I'd heard the night of the Klan rally on our yard? Now I measured every voice against those I'd heard that night. Everyone was suspect. No one was a friend. The familiar blue feeling crept back in.

"As a matter of fact," I said, not looking at him as I cut my papers' wires, "no."

"I'm still looking for him, you know," Miller fumed. "Just because you got off the hook doesn't mean he will."

I stared at him hard. "I didn't get off the hook," I said evenly in a real man's voice, not the pretend one I'd used on Reginald Jones. "I didn't do anything wrong to begin with."

"Huh!" He put his hands on his hips. "Don't think I don't know it was you in that bank talking to Bernard Peterson. You used a made-up name, remember? Mine!" His face was red with anger, his heavy jowls trembling with rage. So that was it—he couldn't stand the idea that a kid like me would use his good name. Despite myself, I laughed.

Raising the papers into my webbed carrier, I brushed past him. "I like my own name better," I said without looking at him. "Yours is too plain!"

He didn't follow me, but I could feel his gaze penetrating my back. It didn't matter. I'd meant what I said. I didn't care what my name said about where I came from. I liked it. I felt like shouting it at the next passer-by. "Yeah, I'm Carl Matuski! That's right—Matuski! You don't like it, you fight me, right here, right now."

I'd never feel ashamed of my name again. I didn't hide it under white hoods and ghostly sheets. I wore it proudly.

My paper route was slow that day, because I was still recovering, and I had to stop once to let a coughing spell pass. I'd be glad when this sickness was done with. I still woke up with night sweats and fever, even though the worst of the illness was gone.

At home, Pete still took care of me by fixing special foods. That night, he made a lamb stew and asked me often about how I was feeling. When I didn't say much, he asked me specifically how many times I'd coughed that day. Clearing the table, he told me to get a lot of rest. "And if you're not any better in a week, I'm having the doctor look at you again," he said.

Pete himself was haggard from work, taking care of me, and his Truth Society meetings. He always had dark shadows under his eyes now, and he looked even thinner than usual, his belt pulled in another notch. He didn't say anything about the story in the paper on the Peterson death, but he did cut out a copy of the Klan rally story. I caught him staring at it and sighing before I went to bed.

Chapter Twenty-One

I had hoped that the Peterson story would take care of every-thing, including removing the pressure on my brother. As Vincent Briggs reported, Peterson had been in debt and doing desperate things to pay it off. He was stealing from his employer, after all. It wasn't unreasonable to think he might have stolen his own mother's jewelry, too. From the start, I'd had a bunch of other suspects—the younger Peterson brother, the maid, the cook, even some random thief—but all that was just speculation. Bernard Peterson had access to the jewels and good reason to steal them. It had to be him.

But there was no clear evidence of it. No one had seen him with the jewelry. No one had heard him talking about them. And they hadn't yet turned up, as far as I knew. This nagged at me.

I still held out hope, though, and kept waiting for more jew-elers to answer the letters I'd written. If Bernard had pawned the jewels, I'd find out eventually and the entire case would be closed.

Later that week, as I sat at the kitchen table finishing a hot cup of strong tea, I tried to think of ways to get that information. Maybe I needed to write to more jewelers and more pawn shops. Or maybe I should go in person.

But what if Peterson had sold the jewels to a private individual? In that case, they'd be nearly impossible to find. Or what if they hadn't been sold yet at all, and were still among his personal belongings? If so, his wife would surely turn them over to Rose's mother. And then Adam would be in the clear.

At the thought of Rose, I sighed. Her sadness must have been acute. Her brother was not only dead but dishonored.

A steady knock at the front door startled me. Pete was at a meeting, so I stood to see who it was, afraid it could be Officer Miller or some other bad sort. "Who's there?" I called out.

"It's me—Vinnie," came the reply. *Vincent Briggs!* What was he doing here? My face breaking into a smile, I opened the door.

Briggs stepped inside at my invitation, shivering in the cool air.

"Geez, you're hard to find, kid. You don't have a telephone?" He looked around our bare living room. For a moment, I was embarrassed. Briggs's house was filled with furniture. It was clean and bright, and looked well cared-for. Our living room held an old sofa with threadbare arms, some spindly chairs, and a broken table propped against the wall.

"Uh . . . come on in, Mr. Briggs," I said, wondering how to treat a visitor. "Want some tea . . . or coffee?"

He followed me to the kitchen table, where I cleared my cup. But he held up a hand to get me to stop.

"I'm not going to stay long. Just wanted to drop something off." After pulling off leather gloves, he dug into his coat pocket, searching for something. "I had to go to Payroll to get your address, but I'm not the paper's best reporter for nothing. I know where to find the facts." After rummaging around for a few seconds, pulling out odd scraps of paper, a thumb tack, a box of matches, and a handkerchief, he finally located what he was looking for. "And other things," he said, holding it up in the light.

A circle of pearly beads in groups of ten—my mother's

rosary!

"The police had it and I managed to get it from them," he said, holding it out to me. "It looked to be a little damaged—a link was missing—but I figured you'd still want it, so I got it fixed for you."

The beads dangled before me. My mother's rosary had been her last gift to me. I never thought I'd see it again. I wanted to hug old Briggs, or jump for joy, or something. But instead, I just stared at it, feeling choked and dry. I took it from him.

"I . . . I don't know how to thank you," I sputtered.

"Thank me? I should be thanking you!" he laughed. "My editor's still shaking his head over how I got that Peterson story!" He looked at me with twinkling eyes that quickly turned serious. "How's that cold of yours?"

"Getting better, sir."

"Stop that 'sir' business, Carl. You can call me Vincent, or you can call me Briggs—anything but Vinnie." He looked around the kitchen. "You getting enough to eat? Who takes care of you?"

I told him about my uncle and where he was, and how I'd be going to the doctor the next week if I didn't get better. I remembered the money Vincent had given me, too. It was still under my mattress. I'd have to give it to Pete.

"Well, if there's anything I can ever do for you, you let me know, young man," Vincent said. He smiled and I could tell he was getting ready to go.

"There *is* one thing," I said. "I'm still trying to find out where those jewels went—what Peterson did with them, that is. I was thinking of getting in touch with jewelers, more jewelers, and I need some help with that. I thought maybe—"

He cut me off. "I'm sorry, Carl. I don't think Bernard Peterson took them. Knowing your brother's problem, I thought about that angle. I figured the jewels would turn up soon. But they haven't."

He rocked back on his heels and let that sink in.

"Who do you think took them, then?" I asked.

Shrugging, he smiled sadly. "I don't know. And I don't know if we'll ever know." He tapped me on the head with his gloves. "You've got a bright future ahead of you, Carl. Don't let distractions weigh you down. Come by and see me at the newsroom whenever you want—especially if you have a good story."

After seeing him to the door, I pulled out my mother's rosary and looked at it for a long time. Then I placed it in my pocket, fingering the smooth beads. In the silence of the house, the nagging thoughts I'd had about the jewels not turning up crystallized into a theory, one I'd been reluctant to face. Peterson had been stealing money from the bank. That was a big risk. It would have been far easier—far less risky—for him to have taken the jewels from his mother's house. They were worth an awful lot. But if he'd taken them, he wouldn't have needed to steal from the bank. He either didn't think of it, or couldn't bring himself to steal from his own mother. He chose the riskier path, stealing from the bank.

What did all that mean?

I kept waiting for the jewels to turn up, hoping they'd provide the last clue I needed. I looked at the newspaper every day, expecting a story about how some petty thief was caught with the jewels on his person. And I kept waiting for Esther to write me again. At least I could do something about that discomfort. I penned another note to her, telling her I'd be back in Baltimore for sure—before Christmas.

The next week, Pete took me to see Doc Beckel, who said I was in the ending stages of pneumonia. He said I was lucky to be doing as well as I was, given the fact I'd hardly let myself recover. I nearly asked him to take a look at Pete, who was as pasty as a ghost and thin as a stick.

I had just about given up on clearing Adam. He wasn't around any more, and now I hoped he'd gotten away—maybe with Lillian. At least then he'd be safe. I liked to think he was turning his life around. *I looked after him as best I could, Ma.*

I thought about trying one more time to interest Vincent Briggs in the case. At least a big newspaper reporter would get some response from jewelers, while my letters had elicited hardly any answers at all.

But that changed the following Monday.

When I came home from the Academy that day, I planned to eat some bread and have a cup of tea, then head out on my paper route. But on the kitchen table was the day's mail, brought in by Pete earlier. He was out in the alley, burning some trash.

There were three letters, each with the return address of one of the jewelry stores I'd written to.

Racing up to my room, I slammed the door behind me and ripped at the first envelope. Down below, Pete's voice called to me, "Carl, there's some chicken on the table. I have to go out!"

"Thanks!" I yelled down to him through the door.

My heart pounding, I growled in frustration as my stubby fingers struggled to grip the fine paper of the first letter tightly enough to open it without tearing it to pieces. I grabbed a pencil on the floor and slipped it into the tiniest crack where the envelope wasn't completely glued, and ripped it open. Tissue-thin paper fluttered out into my hands.

"Dear Mr. Baguette . . ." the letter began. I could hardly see straight, I was so excited, but that was short-lived. ". . . I'm sorry to say," the letter continued, "we do not have any items like the ones you describe in stock. We specialize in fine diamonds and gold. I'd be happy to make a special appointment to show you our inventory should you come this way . . ."

Maybe the next one, I thought, again using the pencil as letter opener. Heavy linen stock fell from this one, but the message was the same—"We do not carry much jewelry at all any longer. Fine watches make up the majority of our stock. We have some lovely ruby-encrusted pocket watches . . ."

I let that letter slip from my hands as I sank onto the bed. *One more.* With less enthusiasm and haste, I slit open this one, from Pendleton Fine Jewels. Another piece of heavy linen paper slid out of the envelope. Expecting more of the same, I straightened as I read:

"Dear Mr. Baguette: We recently acquired an exquisite set of ladies' jewelry that could be just what you are seeking. It is so lovely, in fact, that words cannot describe the fine workmanship and stones. But let me try . . ."

The description was perfect: a diamond bracelet, a pearl pin, and a couple pairs of ruby earrings—exactly what the Petersons were missing! I jumped up and shouted, "Eureka!" I wished Adam were there to see the note. I wanted to find him, to say, "See, if only you'd had more faith. I knew we'd do it. Don't give up. Don't give up on yourself, Adam!"

I wished Vincent were there, too, and Pete, and even Lillian. I wanted to share the news with everyone. I wanted the world to know, especially those white-robed clowns who'd littered our lawn weeks ago.

It was only a matter of time now before Adam would be cleared, just as I had been cleared. Maybe he'd get a sense of his old self back.

Maybe we could go home together.

I thought of my Baltimore friends and how surprised they'd be to see me. Would Billy still be in school? Julian was—Esther had told me so in her letter. If he wanted to be president, he had to study hard, and he'd even talked of trying for college.

Dancing a little jig while I worked, I scooped up the other letters and tossed them under my pillow. I stuffed the Pendleton letter back into its envelope and stuck it in my shirt pocket, next to my heart. My brother was cleared! My brother was cleared! Good things came your way if you were good enough. I had been, and soon, his name cleared, Adam would be, too.

Skipping downstairs, I went into the kitchen and ate like I hadn't eaten in weeks. My appetite expanded as my worries receded.

I still had to identify the jewels, of course, and I would, but first, I had to take off for my paper route. I rushed through it at record speed, thinking all the while how to find Adam. All I needed was for him to identify the jewels, to tell me they were the Peterson valuables. He'd been staying with Lillian at her boarding house near the speakeasy. I didn't have the exact address, but if I headed in that direction, maybe I could ask around.

I'd find the two of them. We were almost in the clear.

Chapter Twenty-Two

Not even bothering to sell my last five copies of the paper, I headed immediately to Lillian's neighborhood. It reminded me of ours, with old homes in desperate need of paint jobs and repairs. Spotting a bent-over man walking ahead, I stopped and asked about Lillian, describing her flame-red hair, which made her easy to remember. The fellow pointed to a peeling gray house near the corner, where, at the door, a young woman greeted me. She looked sleepy and her hair was a bush of frizzy curls.

"I'm looking for Lillian," I said.

Without even asking who I was, she let me in and pointed upstairs. "Number three," she said before vanishing down a dim hallway and behind another door.

Upstairs, I knocked gently on Lillian's door, but no one answered. Turning the knob slowly so it wouldn't squeak, I opened the door. The shades were drawn, so the room was darkened by late afternoon shadows. A flowery scent hit my nose, triggering a cough. The noise stirred a figure asleep on the mussed bed—Adam.

He rolled over and stared at me.

"What are you doing here?" he asked, sitting up.

His beard was bristly, and his hair was dirty. Because he'd been sleeping fully-clothed, his shirt was wrinkled—stained, too. I'd wanted to find him, all right. But I'd wanted to find him *changed*.

"I thought you'd left town," I said.

"Tonight," he said, stretching. "I was going to get the ticket now." He stood.

"Just you? Not Lillian, too?"

"Oh," he said, as if he'd forgotten something. "Yeah, sure. I need to get a ticket for her, too. She gave me the money." He patted his pocket, making sure it was still there.

"Before you leave, I need you to do something," I said. "I need you to go with me to Pendleton Jewelers around Irvington."

"Wha . . . why?"

"They have the jewels, Adam. They have the stolen jewels. They'll know who brought them in."

He didn't respond. He looked down and then away. He folded his arms across his chest.

"I have to catch this train, Carl. I can't go."

"But Adam," I said, "this could clear you."

He chuckled softly. "It doesn't matter. I'm leaving anyway."

"Listen, Adam," I said, fingering the hem of my jacket, "it's going to be over soon—this whole awful nightmare. I know how you feel. I felt the same way when it looked like they could go after me for Peterson's death. It's like the whole world wants to hem you in. I know, Adam! I know!"

He stared at me but didn't say anything. I saw him redden, as if I'd embarrassed him. The old Adam was still hidden deep within—hidden under an invisible white robe all his own—but there *was* still good underneath, waiting to be rediscovered.

"Adam, I didn't give up. And you shouldn't, either. Please, come with me to the jeweler's."

He just shook his head slowly. "Carl, it would be a waste of time," he said.

I waited, hoping he'd change his mind, but he said nothing.

"When's your train leave?" I asked at last.

Reflexively, he patted his pocket, looking for our father's watch.

"The watch is on your bed at Pete's. It fell out of your pocket," I said.

"I was wondering," he answered. "Couldn't find it for days."

"You want me to get it?" I asked. But, if I did, I might return to find him already gone. "Why don't you come by and get it yourself?" I added.

"My train leaves at six o'clock—sleeper to San Francisco, then on to Chicago."

I looked around the room. Silky women's undergarments lay on a dresser. A scarf was tied on the edge of a mirror. Cheap jewelry spilled out of a box, and a stocking was draped over the edge of a drawer. "Is Lillian meeting you at the station?"

"Yeah, that's right." Following my gaze to the disorder in the room, he gestured to a tapestry bag in the corner. "I . . . I'm supposed to pack her things for her."

I didn't ask if they were married. I was beginning to realize there were things about my brother I'd rather not know. One thing I *did* know—I could stand there until the sun set and rose again and Adam would not agree to go to the jeweler with me. He'd given up. I'd have to find another way to identify those jewels and determine who took them.

"Write to me," I said at last. "Tell me where you end up."

"Sure, kid." He didn't move. Placing his hands in his pockets, he looked sheepishly at the floor. "Sorry about all the trouble."

"Yeah, well . . . it'll all be fine, once we get to Baltimore."

"You know, Portland's not that bad a place," he added. "Lots of opportunities here. Lots of ways to make it on your own."

"It's not like home," I said, suddenly on edge. What was he

really saying?

"Pete's tried to make a home for you."

"But Baltimore is where—"

"You could make friends here," he snapped. "You just haven't tried." Then he laughed. "You certainly don't need me dragging you down."

What was he saying? Suddenly, he wanted me to stay here, as if it was for my own good. Adam had always looked out for me, or at least I thought he had, but now it felt more like he was trying to fool me than help me. Did he not want me to come with him? Did he think I'd drag him down?

Another line from Esther's letter jumped back into my head. She had asked where Adam was. She assumed he wasn't with me, but at the same time, she knew of our Uncle Pete, because Adam had told Julian's sister about him. What could Adam have said? It must have been that we were heading to Pete's . . . and Adam wasn't staying.

Adam had planned to leave me with Uncle Pete. He never meant to stay and take care of me—he was just waiting to get enough cash to get out. He might as well have punched me in the gut.

And he'd never even told me.

I looked at him now, trying to see the brother I once knew, the fellow who'd looked out for me, the Adam who would have punched out anyone who tried to hurt me. But what I once saw as bravery, I now recognized as bluster. What I once saw as pride, I now realized was swagger that concealed fear. He'd never been the hero I envisioned. He was just a boy forced to grow up too soon.

"Stop by the house and get your watch before you go," I repeated softly. Suddenly, I wanted to be out of this lilac-scented room. "And don't worry, Adam. I'm fine on my own."

We wished each other quiet goodbyes and I left.

I didn't know why at first, but I headed to the newspaper office after seeing Adam. Vincent Briggs had said to stop by anytime, and I *did* have the jeweler's letter to show him now. Maybe he could help me. More than that, though, Vincent Briggs was a friend. And I needed to talk to a friend after saying goodbye to Adam.

As I walked into town, I wondered if I'd ever see my brother again. It certainly sounded like he was ready never to see me. Shoving my hands into my pocket, I kicked stones and kept my head down. It was all too late.

Vincent Briggs was still at his desk when I arrived, though every other reporter had left for the day. He smiled broadly when he saw me, and stared at the jeweler's letter for a long time after I gave it to him. Tapping his cigar-laden hand on the desk, he spoke to the air in front of him more than to me. "Someone from the Peterson family," he said. "They'd have to identify the jewels. And then we could find out who sold them."

"Rose," I offered. "Bernard's sister. She might do it." Poor Rose. I wished I could see her again, but at the same time, Adam and I had caused her so much trouble and sorrow.

Briggs whirled his chair toward me. "You sure you want to know?"

What a curious question! Of course I wanted to know. I still wanted to clear Adam. I still wanted to prove to the world he was no crook. And on top of that, I wanted to prove I was no vagabond. I could finish what I started. Squaring my shoulders, I stared into Briggs's eyes.

"Yes."

After scrambling through some papers, he found the Peterson

phone number and placed the call. Rose Peterson agreed to meet him at the jeweler's. "It might give your mother some peace of mind," Vincent said.

After finishing the call, he reached for his hat and coat on a nearby rack. Standing, he grabbed the letter from his desk and folded it, placing it in his pocket.

"Alfred Baguette, eh?" He laughed. "If you don't mind, I'll tell the jeweler Mr. Baguette sent me. I prefer my own name."

As we left the now-quiet building, Briggs asked if I wanted to come, but I wasn't sure I could even look at Rose, knowing I could have done more to save her brother. So Briggs told me he'd drive me home and come by later with whatever news he'd found.

"At least it'll be settled one way or another," he said after a silent drive to my door.

Settled one way or another. Something else bothered me. What had Adam said when I'd asked him to go to the jewelers? *It would be a waste of time.* I cleaned up the kitchen for Pete, and made a pot of coffee for when Vincent came by. I tried to stay busy. But thoughts kept intruding. I went over the case. Adam, Bernard, and Jonesy were all deeply entangled with the gambling ring. They were all desperate. Each had been on the lam one way or another, trying to get themselves out of debt. Bernard and Jonesy used the bank. Jonesy even tried blackmail.

And what had Adam done to get himself out of the gang's clutches? Probably borrowed money from Lillian, maybe even from Rose before the trouble over the jewels began. Would it have been enough? Lillian had said he was still in debt.

An hour later, I was upstairs in my bedroom, still thinking all this through, facing facts I'd not wanted to see clearly before. I heard the front door open below. Figuring it was Pete, I didn't get up. I didn't know what I'd tell him when Vincent Briggs stopped by later.

But when footsteps sounded into the old bedroom I'd shared with Adam, I straightened and went into the hallway.

"Who's there?" I called out. "Pete?"

Silence, followed by, "It's me, Adam. Just came by to get a few things."

Adam! There were so many things I wanted to say to him. I was angrier than ever at how he'd deceived me, making me think he wanted to go back to Baltimore with him when all he really wanted was to be rid of the burden of caring for his younger brother.

Adam was soon scooping up his pocket watch and the few pieces of clothing he'd left behind. He walked fast between rooms, looking for items he might have left, and anything of value he could find. He threw everything into a rumpled sack.

In his rummaging, he found the money Vincent Briggs had given me at the coffee shop to give to Pete. "This yours?" he asked, a note of suspicion creeping into his voice. He thought I'd held out on him. We stood in the hallway, eye to eye.

"Yeah."

He looked at the wad of money, then at me, but didn't hand over the cash. He was going to ask me to "lend" it to him. But before I'd even consider doing that, he'd have to answer a few questions.

"Adam, I need to ask you . . ." I heard a knock at the front door. I let it delay me. I didn't want to ask Adam the question. It would produce an unpleasant answer either way—a lie or a painful truth. Holding up my hand, I stared at Adam, daring him to leave. "Wait! Just a minute. Please! This won't take long."

After running downstairs, I opened the door to Vincent Briggs. I looked over his shoulder to see if anyone was with him. He shook his head. "I took Rose home already—wasn't far from the jeweler's." For a fleeting second, hope returned. If the jeweler was close to the Peterson home, maybe it was because Bernard had sold the items there. Maybe he had stolen them, after all, and I could discard my new theory.

"They weren't the Peterson jewels," he said brusquely. My fears were confirmed.

Standing just inside the door, he didn't even bother to take off his gloves. "They were completely different. Only one ruby in the set. The jeweler thought he could convince me to buy them instead of the ones 'Mr. Baguette' said he was looking for." He scowled. "Rose was quite upset."

Dropping onto the step, I sat with my head in my hands. More pain for Rose. How callous I'd become! "I . . . I'm sorry. I'll have to tell her so . . ."

"You're a good investigator, Carl," Briggs said. "You were trying to follow every lead."

I'd been on a fool's errand, trying to clear my brother.

Adam—I heard him moving upstairs.

Then I heard something else, sending icy fear through my spine. Voices carried from outside. One was Pete's, but the other was Officer Miller's.

". . . saw him coming this way," Miller was saying.

"If he's here, I'll have him talk to you," Pete said in an angry voice.

I stared wide-eyed at Briggs. "Wait here just a minute. I have to . . . do something."

I raced up the stairs to Adam, who was searching his room for any stray bits of change. He'd pocketed the cash I'd not yet agreed to lend him, I realized with a wince.

"Turn yourself in!" I whispered to him. By now, I could hear Pete and Officer Miller entering the house. Their voices were a confused jumble as Briggs introduced himself. Officer Miller asked for me as well, but Briggs said he wasn't sure where I was. Adam looked frantic and retied his bundle.

"Maybe he's upstairs," Pete said to Miller. "He's been sickly lately, you know." Pete's voice boomed up to me, "Carl! Are you up there? Get up, son! . . . He's probably resting," I heard him say.

"Coming!" I yelled back weakly, but I stayed where I was. "Turn yourself in, Adam," I repeated. "They'll go easier on you if you do."

Adam looked frantically at the door, then back at me. "You, too, huh?" he said, as if I'd betrayed him. Downstairs, Pete was again calling my name.

"Be right there!" I yelled downstairs. Then, to Adam, I said, "Bernard and Jonesy both did desperate things to keep out of the gambling ring's debt. What did you do, Adam?"

"Not enough," he said. "They're still after me. Look, I gotta go."

"You knew it was a waste of time to go to the jewelers. You knew the jewels still hadn't been pawned," I said.

Adam said nothing.

"You were waiting for things to quiet down before you pawned them," I continued.

"I'm in big trouble here," Adam said, self-pity in his voice. "You gotta help me get away. Didn't I always help you, Carl?"

"I'll help you give yourself up. Do it now, Adam. There's no time."

He didn't answer. Then, in a blur of motion, he brushed past me to the hallway, knocking me into the door. While he headed for the window in the back room, I scrambled to get up and follow him. Already he was at the window.

"Adam!" I called, no longer caring if they heard me downstairs.

Adam was easing his right leg out the window, his bundle dangling over the ledge.

A commotion came from downstairs as Pete and Miller rushed up.

Adam dropped to the ground as I came to the window. Just as he grabbed his bundle, something slipped from it, hitting the concrete with a dull little clink. He looked down at it and so did I.

From the light spilling out of the kitchen window, the item sparkled, like a deep-red marble surrounded by shiny stones. On the gray concrete, it looked like a drop of blood.

It was an earring.

My heart seemed to follow it there, hitting the ground with a crash and shattering, alongside my faith in Adam. As my heart broke, it cut open other truths. Here was the evidence to confirm my last theory—the only one I was right about. Adam had done it. He'd taken the jewelry. And then, I realized, Adam had shown up at the house without Lillian's bag. She wasn't going to meet him at the station. He was planning to run off without her. He probably took her money the way he'd taken mine.

He *was* a thief.

My brother was a thief and a gambler and, for all I knew, he had been the same back in Baltimore.

My mouth fell open and time stopped. Adam's face turned up toward me, his eyes narrowing and his mouth gaping wide as he realized what I'd seen. I heard footsteps on the stairs. There was no time—no time for explanations, no time for excuses.

"Please, Carl," Adam whispered. "Don't tell them."

I said nothing. The ruby earring had me hypnotized. The footsteps behind me got closer, and I stayed frozen, staring at that earring.

"You told me . . ." I started to say.

"I told you to stop investigating!" Adam said from the yard. His voice was shrill and hurt. "I loved Rose. I really did," he continued, "but her parents wouldn't accept me. I needed the money. I knew they had the jewelry."

"We were going to go home to Baltimore together," I said, more to myself than to him. By now, I knew that had never been his dream, only mine. He'd let me latch onto it while he made other plans.

"You don't need me, kid!" Adam whispered. "You never really did!" And then he laughed, just the way he used to. "Look at all you've done on your own. Bollixed everything up for me, solving this case." He smiled at me and waved.

"Carl! Who you talking to?" Officer Miller's voice came from the hallway. "Is that him?"

Turning around, I saw Miller walking down the shadowy hall, huffing and puffing after coming up the stairs. Vincent Briggs and Pete weren't far behind.

"Is that him?" said Miller, his voice shaking with anger. But I was frozen again, not knowing what to do or say, thinking about what Adam had just said. He'd really loved Rose, but her parents hated him, a boy from the wrong side of town. That had sounded true.

Something collapsed inside of me as I thought of how he must have felt when he realized they hated him because of who he came into the world as, not who he was or what he could do. I remembered the night of the burning cross, when the Klansmen had gathered on our yard looking for Adam. Pete had stood up to them, defying them. He'd refused to surrender Adam to them.

I remembered something Pete had said to me many days ago: "If Adam's done something bad, it's not because he's a Catholic or the son of Poles." That's why Pete had stood up to the Klan.

They'd wanted to drag Adam off because he was Catholic.

"Was that him?" Officer Miller repeated, pointing toward the window. I looked at him and then at Vincent. Vincent must have guessed. When he'd figured out Bernard Peterson probably hadn't taken the jewels, he'd also come to the most obvious conclusion. That's why Vincent had asked me if I was sure I wanted to know who took the jewels. He knew the truth would hurt me.

I looked at Pete, whose pale face showed worry and anger. He knew, too. They all had known—except me, until now. I'd believed in Adam. I'd thought he was innocent, a victim of hate-filled souls who wanted to brand him guilty.

He *was* guilty, but not because of his name or his religion.

Weakly pointing to the place where my once-beloved brother had escaped, I said softly, "He's headed to the train station."

Reversing course, Miller turned and ran down the stairs, through the house, and out the back door. I could hear him racing up the alley, but Adam's footsteps were gone. He had a long stride and was fresh from resting. Miller was heavier, and always looked used up. Adam would get away, at least for now.

The three of us—Vincent, Pete, and I—stood in my bedroom listening to the footfalls die away outside. At last, Vincent spoke. "You did the right thing," he said.

Pete stepped forward and touched me on the shoulder.

"There's some milk in the icebox," he said, "and it might still have the cream on top. Help yourself."

"Thanks," I muttered, hurrying to the door so they wouldn't see my face, damp with tears.

Epilogue

They caught Adam before he left Portland.

Officer Miller called headquarters, which had another policeman intercept Adam at the train station.

Within a month, he was before a judge. I didn't understand everything that happened, but I do know he managed to avoid jail by handing over the items he stole. Rose helped there, telling the judge she "gave" the jewels to Adam for safekeeping the night they went to the speakeasy together.

Poor Rose must have felt bad about her parents not liking Adam. Or maybe she knew from her own brother's sad fate just how horrible that gambling ring had been, and didn't want any more people to suffer because of it. Whatever her reasoning, I felt sorry for her and wished I could tell her so. Adam had betrayed her, just as he'd betrayed me. But talking to Rose would have meant talking about her brother's death, something I felt my own share of guilt about. I'd write her about it someday. It was something I had to work up to.

The following week, Pete, his anger fearsome, came home and told me the people had spoken on Election Day, making it illegal for anybody to go to St. Mary's Academy, or anything but a public school. He broke a glass in the sink and let out a string of Polish curses I'd never heard before. He took a bottle of vodka he had hidden in a cabinet and downed a quick glass before heading to the house of the Petrovich widow. He didn't return until late that night, and told me in the morning that he and the Petrovich woman were going to get married.

As for me, I picked up other odd jobs and added to my store of savings. Within another month, I had enough to head back to Baltimore—not by much, but I would make good on my promise to Esther to be home before Christmas. Before leaving Portland, I heard from her again, and she repeated her offer of a place to stay.

East! Back to Baltimore! I'd always looked forward to making the journey with Adam, and hadn't thought myself capable of doing it on my own. Now I planned the trip all alone, confident I could handle it.

When I went to the paper to tell Briggs, he took his cigar out of his mouth, shook his head, and, for a few moments, said nothing. Then he grabbed his hat and coat and took me downtown to Meier and Frank's, where he bought me a brown wool muffler and gloves as a "bon voyage" present. He shook my hand real hard when he said goodbye, and told me to keep in touch. And he promised to write a letter of recommendation for me to give to any Baltimore newspaper, in case I decided to go into the business.

I got the letter in the mail a couple days later. It made me feel proud and funny at the same time. Briggs had written lots of great things about me—how smart and good I was—things I'd never heard anyone but Ma say about me before.

Pete was sad to hear I was leaving, and I was surprised when he gave me a big hug goodbye. I told him to come visit me and promised I'd do the same. But with the distance and the expense, I think we both knew those visits were dreams that would fade over time. We'd always write, though.

A week after that, as I sat in the big station waiting for my train, I fingered Vincent's letter in my pocket, afraid I'd lose it if

I didn't keep it close. I pulled it out and read it from time to time because it cheered me when I started thinking about Adam too much. I couldn't hold a grudge against Adam, though, even after all he'd done. His plan might have been to take me to Uncle Pete and then go off on his own, but he never really did. Maybe it was because he didn't have the money, but maybe he just couldn't abandon me. That's why he'd stayed in Portland. For all his troubles, there was still some goodness buried within him.

I didn't know where he'd gone once the judge set him free. He didn't move back in with Pete, and probably Lillian didn't want him, either, given the fact he'd planned on leaving town without her. Maybe with his debt left to pay and those loan enforcers after him, he just picked up his things, caught the first train out, and left for good. Maybe I'd hear from him someday. Maybe, sooner or later, he'd show up in Baltimore. Wherever he ended up, I believed Adam could put together a life for himself. I hoped *he* did, too.

Movement by the entrance caught my eye and I glanced up just as a lanky fellow about my brother's age walked in with a bag in his hand and bewilderment in his eyes. Scanning the large room, he bit his lip, then squared his shoulders as if getting ready for battle, marching forward with confidence toward the ticket teller. A few seconds later, he was marching in another direction—toward a window where tickets to the California train lines were sold. He pretended to be confident, but I could tell he was scared.

There was the picture of the brother I used to know—or thought I'd known. He'd always reassured me everything would be all right, all the while not knowing what the future held.

Everything *would* be all right, I thought, when my train was finally called. I shifted my bag onto my shoulder.

I was going home.

Notes on This Book

Among the resources I used to write this story was *The State and the Non-Public School* by Lloyd Jorgenson (University of Missouri Press).

I also made use of Catholic University of America's resources on the Oregon School law, including:

* Archbishop Christie's Pastoral Letter
* Memories of the Ku Klux Klan in La Grande, Oregon
* Minutes of a Ku Klux Klan meeting
* *The Old Cedar School*
* Archbishop Christie's letter to the National Catholic Welfare Conference
* The Oregon school law referendum question
* *The New Catholic Encyclopedia: Oregon School Case*

My book's reference to "Sister Lucretia, the escaped nun" comes from the Jorgenson book, which reports, "The Klan's revival of the favorite nativist weapon against the Roman Church [was] the 'escaped nun.' Sister Lucretia was paraded about the state, sometimes appearing in public school auditoriums, to vilify Catholicism in general." A previous "escaped nun," who'd appeared in the mid-1800s as a weapon against Catholics, had been examined by medical doctors and declared insane.

Elsa Richter, the teacher in this book who is thrown out of teaching at a Portland public school because of pressure from the Klan, is fictional.

However, Margaret Myers of La Grande, Oregon (who was ten at the time of the Oregon School vote) has recorded memories of her aunt, Evelyn Newlin, being fired as an eighth-grade teacher in a public school because "the Newlins sent their children to the Catholic school." After that, Newlin was given a job teaching at the parish school.

Minutes of a Ku Klux Klan meeting during the time confirm the Klan's antipathy toward Newlin. When a petition was circulated to reinstate her, the Klan minutes reported that the petition "is thouroughly [sic] un-American, a direct insult to the School Bill; and Something that the Klan will not under any Consideration tolerate if in their power . . . This women [sic] not only sends her children to the Paroical [sic] School but her Influnce [sic] with the pupils in her charge is not born of old Glory; neither is it symbolic of the firey [sic] Cross. I have taken particular pains to find the originator of this petition and it is no other than her husband Mr. Chester Newlin; the Esteemed Gentleman who sat at the polls and told our worthy citizens how to vote the right way. I sincerely believe that this town could run very well without citizens by the Name Bearing the Title of Newlin . . ."

Newlin's niece, Margaret Myers, later became a Sister of the Holy Names of Jesus and Mary.

The Klan gatherings in this novel are fictional, but the large gathering involving an electric cross is loosely based on a real gathering that took place in the Pacific Northwest several years later.

The quoted excerpts from *The Old Cedar School* book are real.

The St. Mary's Academy in the novel is real, as is the order of nuns who ran it. They were instrumental in filing the lawsuit that eventually overturned the law. In fact, the U.S. Supreme Court case bears their name: *Pierce vs. Society of Sisters*.

The Oregon School Law and Anti-Catholicism

After the Communist revolution in Russia and the end of World War I, some Americans began to fear that outsiders might attempt to radically change the American way of life. In particular, immigrants, especially Catholic immigrants, were viewed as potential troublemakers. Most Americans at the time were Protestants.

One way to control outside influences on American life was to control the education of children. Ever since the beginning of the public school movement in the mid-1800s, some people wanted to use public schools to neutralize or eliminate what they considered to be threatening "papist" views held by Catholic immigrant children.

Early public schools, however, were not free of religion. They were drenched in non-denominational Christian instruction in which children were taught to sing Protestant hymns, say Protestant prayers, and read the Protestant version of the Bible (the King James version rather than the Catholic Douay version). If children didn't participate, they were punished, sometimes severely. This religious intolerance was the reason Catholics built their own schools—it was to make sure Catholic children wouldn't be forced to participate in religious activities they didn't embrace.

As the parochial system of education grew in America, so did tension between zealous nativists and Catholics.

In the early 1920s, movements in Michigan, California, Texas, Oklahoma, Ohio, Wyoming, Arkansas, and Nebraska arose to pass laws making it illegal to send children to anything but a public school. Those efforts were not successful.

In the fall of 1922, Oregon voters were asked to decide

whether sending children to a private school in Oregon should become illegal. The campaign for this law was led by members of the Ku Klux Klan and other groups whose members believed that Catholics and foreigners were bad influences on American society. Catholic schools in particular, and private schools in general, were a threat to democracy, they believed. In their view, Catholic children were "mongrels" who had to be "Americanized" by going through the public school system.

In fact, the King Kleagle of the Pacific Ku Klux Klan believed Americans were facing "the ultimate perpetuation or destruction of free institutions, based upon the perpetuation or destruction of the public schools."

In other words, if you didn't send your children to public schools and support them, you were un-American.

One of the supporters of the law was the Democratic candidate for governor in Oregon, Walter M. Pierce, who asked for and received the support of the Klan during his campaign. He won the election.

Supporters of the Oregon law circulated anti-Catholic pamphlets such as *The Old Cedar School*, which portrayed Catholics not just as destroyers of public schools, but as people who believed in strange rituals and bizarre religious theories. (Sections of *The Old Cedar School* quoted in this book are real.)

Although the Oregon School Law was anti-Catholic, no major Protestant church endorsed the law. No public school leaders supported it, either.

On November 7, 1922, by a vote of 115,506 to 103,685, Oregon voters approved the school measure that required parents to send children between the ages of eight and sixteen to public schools only. If parents disobeyed by sending their children to private schools, they would have to pay a daily fine, face imprisonment, or both.

A year later, the law was challenged in court, and the case eventually made its way to the U.S. Supreme Court. On June 1, 1925, the court ruled unanimously that the Oregon law was unconstitutional. In their ruling, the justices wrote:

> *The fundamental theory of liberty upon which all governments in this Union repose excludes any general power of the state to standardize its children by forcing them to accept instruction from public teachers only. The child is not the mere creature of the state; those who nurture him and direct his destiny have the right coupled with the high duty to recognize and prepare him for additional obligations.*

In this ruling, the Court said that parents have the right to choose how their children should be educated, and that individual freedom is more important than government-imposed conformity. Nearly 500 newspaper editorials were published in 44 states applauding the High Court's ruling.

Some people believe the ruling influenced the wording of the United Nations Declaration of Human Rights, which says, in part, "Parents have a prior right to choose the kind of education that shall be given to their children."

Possible Discussion Questions

1. What does Pete mean when he tells Carl that if Adam is guilty, it's not because he's a Catholic?

2. Why was the rosary that Carl carried evidence he was a Catholic?

3. Why was Adam guilty?

4. Do you think Adam did bad things because he began to believe immigrants and Catholics were bad?

5. If he began to believe those things, did it justify doing bad things?

6. How did the newspaper reporter Vincent Briggs help Carl?

7. What did Vincent Briggs mean when he told Carl he didn't help anybody except the truth?

8. Why is it important for reporters to uncover the truth?

9. How did Carl's Uncle Pete show that he loved his nephews?

10. Why do you think the people of Oregon passed the School Law? At the time, might it have been the right thing to do?

11. What do you think the U.S. Supreme Court meant when it said "the child is not the mere creature of the State"?

Acknowledgements

As a former education reform activist, I offer my appreciation to all who work in that field, trying to ensure that every child has access to a high quality education, wherever it might be offered.

My sincere thanks also go to the members of the Dorothy L mystery readers and writers group, some of whom helped with information about Portland and its history, and all of whom provide a wonderful forum for mystery aficionados.

Thanks, too, to my sister-in-law, Leslie Lebl, for her encouragement and help with Polish phrases, and to all of my family for their continued support of my writing career.

Finally, a heartfelt thanks to editors Bruce Bortz and Harrison Demchick, who helped me uncover Carl's true character, and whose faith in this story ensures it will be told.

About the Author

Libby Sternberg's first young adult novel, *Uncovering Sadie's Secrets*, was a finalist for the prestigious Edgar Allan Poe award from the Mystery Writers of America. The second in that mystery series, *Finding the Forger*, was released in hardcover in November 2004 (both were published as mass-market paperbacks by Smooch) and a third will be released in 2008. Her debut adult novel, *Loves Me, Loves Me Not* (published under the name Libby Malin) was released in 2005 to critical acclaim.

A Baltimore native, Libby earned both a bachelor's and a master's degree from the Peabody Conservatory of Music and also attended the summer American School of Music in Fontainebleau, France.

After graduating from Peabody, she worked as a Spanish gypsy, a Russian courtier, a Middle-Eastern slave, a Japanese geisha, a Chinese peasant, and a French courtesan—that is, she sang as a union chorister in both the Baltimore and Washington Operas, where she regularly had the thrill of walking through the stage doors of the Kennedy Center Opera House in Washington, D.C. before being costumed and wigged for performance. She also sang with small opera and choral companies in the region.

For many years, she and her family lived in Vermont, where she worked as an education reform advocate promoting school choice policies, contributed occasional commentaries for Vermont Public Radio, and was a member of the Vermont Commission on Women.

She is married, with three children, and now resides in Lancaster, Pennsylvania.

PRAISE FOR
The Case Against My Brother

"A riveting story of faith and betrayal against a background of bigotry. Touching and inspiring."—CAROLYN HART, MYSTERY NOVELIST WIDELY HAILED AS AMERICA'S HEIR TO AGATHA CHRISTIE

"I will admit to a weakness for well-written young adult mysteries, but have rarely found one I consider superior. *The Case Against My Brother* is that very rare exception . . . I highly recommend it—to anyone of any age."—SARAH BEWLEY, AWARD-WINNING PLAYWRIGHT AND SCREENWRITER

"As a Catholic who grew up in an older city neighborhood of mainly eastern Europeans, I found this terrific book to be both touching and highly informative."—MARY SUNDAY, LIBRARIAN, THE CATHOLIC HIGH SCHOOL OF BALTIMORE

"Illuminating a dark corner of American history too often forgotten, it vividly portrays how religious and ethnic intolerance can poison a community and ruin lives . . . Today's children, I hope, will read this book and learn that intolerance wears many disguises, including nationalism."—PAULA ABRAMS, PROFESSOR, LEWIS & CLARK LAW SCHOOL, WHO'S PUBLISHED A LAW REVIEW ARTICLE, AND IS WRITING A BOOK, ON THE OREGON SCHOOL CASE

"An important and entertaining book for both teens and adults."—Dan Lips, education analyst, The Heritage Foundation

"Highly recommended, especially for anyone who likes their mysteries with an historical touch." —Jody Crocker, Library Assistant, Kansas State University Libraries

"Gripping and absorbing."—Theresa de Valence, Mystery Reviewer, Point Richmond, CA

"The Polish American characters are well-drawn, without the gaffs over language and culture that occur so often when outsiders write about an ethnic group, and the sub-plot of anti-Catholicism and prejudice against Poles in America makes important points about America's historical nativism—about which many young readers will no doubt be learning for the first time—without turning the book into a tract. A compelling mystery and a classic coming-of-age story, it is entertaining, enlightening, and important."—Karen Majewski, Ph.D., Executive Director, Polish American Historical Association